HORSES *of the* DAWN

STAR RISE

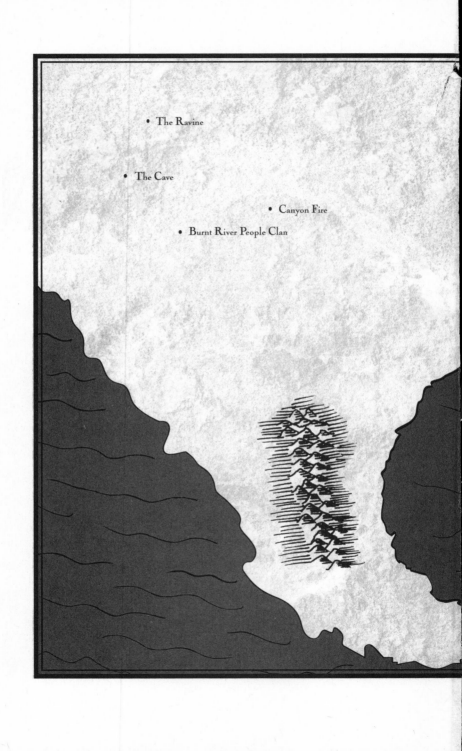

The Ravine

The Cave

Canyon Fire

Burnt River People Clan

HORSES of the DAWN

STAR RISE

KATHRYN LASKY

SCHOLASTIC INC.

Library of Congress Cataloging-in-Publication Data Available

ISBN 978-0-545-39717-9

10 9 8 7 6 5 4 3 2 1   15 16 17 18 19

Printed in the U.S.A.   23

First edition, January 2015

Book design by Whitney Lyle

"Ga' was that most elusive of all owl qualities. It literally meant "great spirit"; a spirit that somehow did not contain only all that is noble but all that is humble, as well."

— From the eleventh book of the Hoolian legends,
To Be a King

The Spirit Trail

The boy watched the old woman's narrow chest. The intervals between her breaths had lengthened, stretching out until they were fewer than the fingers on his hand. She was going Otang — taking the last walk to eternity. That was what the word meant. But was it really walking? Not precisely. It was more that the others walked *away* from the elderly one. Haru had declared her intentions when the people were loading their sledges with their few belongings — hides, baskets, pots, stone implements — to move on to better country.

"I go now on the road to the spirit camps," Haru had announced. "I thank you for the privilege of living with you." The people murmured and commented on her dignity. She shot Tijo a harsh glance. The meaning was clear: *Don't follow me!* However, she knew it was futile. The boy would follow her to the place she had chosen to die.

When their band left, the boy made a show of leaving as well. But soon, Haru picked up the curious beat of his footsteps; the syncopated rhythm of his lame walk always betrayed him.

When he found her, she was sitting cross-legged with her pipe clamped between her remaining teeth. She began making gestures with her hands, signing but not speaking. Her palsied hands shook, making the signs blurry, but Tijo understood them.

These are the rules: You do not speak. You do not bring me food. No water. You do not make me warm by lying next to me, or bringing me your star blanket. I wove that blanket for you. Not me. If the mountain lion comes, you run and let him eat me. Her hands stopped midair and trembled. *And you never say my name or I shall fall off the spirit trail and never reach the spirit camps.*

Tijo nodded solemnly, filled with an odd mixture of feelings. He was sad that she was leaving, but he was grateful that he could be here with her. Haru would not die alone.

He had almost died alone shortly after his birth eleven years before. His crooked leg had condemned him. His mother had died in childbirth, three weeks after his father was killed by a mountain lion. Normally, malformed babies were abandoned, but Haru had saved him. She was powerful within her band. She had been an excellent tracker in her day and knew the stars.

Not only could Haru read the tracks of animals and follow the transit of the stars, she was also known as a smeller of weather. She could smell clouds even before they appeared on the horizon. She was as important in the band as the healer, and many thought her remedies were better than his. Perhaps that was why he'd decided to kill her.

Now as she teetered on the brink between life and death, Haru felt relieved that she had made Tijo promise not to interfere with her passage, a passage that she was sure had been hastened by the healer, for she had felt a numbness in her fingers in the days after the corn silk ceremony. The silk from the corn was put into a fermented brew, and she sensed that her cup had been tainted. Most likely the healer had rubbed her cup with the powder of liverbleed leaves, an almost untraceable poison. The healer was cunning, cunning as a coyote. He could not risk poisoning the brew, for then everyone would die. Though he would hardly have mourned if Tijo had drunk from that pot. Tijo was lame but he was intelligent, and if there was anything the healer feared, it was intelligence. But she would not curse the healer. She would not die with a curse on her lips. If she did, she would be doomed to be a spirit walker and never find the way to the camps of Otang. Nor would she be able to find a spirit lodge on earth, a shelter in the body of a living creature — except of course for the crows, or the vultures. The carrion eaters. She would rather take lodge in a coyote than a carrion eater.

She could feel the boy next to her. She thought she could almost hear his tears rolling down his cheeks. *Don't cry,* she wanted to say. *I am off to a good place.*

Haru had not abandoned him to die alone and Tijo would not abandon her. He dared not even think her name, lest he cause her to fall off the spirit trail.

He looked over at Haru. Would she feel lonely if he were not here? Though he knew it was not so much *her* loneliness he was concerned about but the immutable solitude that death would leave for him, the vacant space that had been Haru in this world.

What would happen to him? He had never been accepted by the members of Haru's clan, the Burnt River People. His twisted leg had forced Haru to hide him for the first month of his life. By the end of one month, a baby was deemed too old to be cast out. But even after the Burnt River People had discovered Haru's secret, Tijo and Haru had lived mostly apart from the clan. He was still shunned, but the people were too dependent on Haru for her knowledge of medicine to totally ignore them.

They looked at him, but never directly into his eyes. If Tijo returned, there would be no one to share a cooking fire with, no one whose breath he would hear through the night as he slept. No one to speak with, no one to learn from, no one to sing with as they scraped the hides for their clothing and blankets.

Tijo would follow the rules, but he would not leave her. Haru would not fall off the spirit trail, and if she did, he would be there to catch her. He might be lame, his one leg crooked and shorter than the other, but he was strong. How heavy could she be? Not much more than the weight of a newborn lamb. He looked over at Haru. Her chest had not risen in a long time. He crept closer. He could not remember when she had taken her last breath, but suddenly she took another. The sound of the air passing through her windpipe was jagged. Her nose twitched. *Does she smell a storm coming?* Tijo wondered.

The smell . . . the smell . . . so different. Goodness, this spirit trail is interesting, Haru thought. There was an animal odor unlike any she had ever known. Not fur but hair. Not human but definitely animal. Heavy of bone, large, very large. Larger than a dog. She felt a flutter of excitement. *So many things on the trail to eternity . . . so many interesting things.* A slight shiver passed through her, as if she were shedding her own pelt. It was a lovely feeling. She was so light. She looked back and saw her body, but it was no more important to her than a discarded blanket, or an animal's pelt she had scraped to make a pair of buckskin trousers for Tijo. She wouldn't need it anymore. She saw Tijo bending over her, weeping. She wanted to reach out and touch that thatch of shiny black hair. *Don't cry. Don't worry.* She wanted to return and soothe him. But there was no going back on the trail of Otang.

If Haru had turned back, she might have been tempted to keep going, for in the immensity of this star-powdered night, Tijo seemed like the tiniest speck of matter in the universe. He looked smaller, more vulnerable than when she had first found him abandoned on the trail side. But she did not turn back. She kept walking toward a pale and inviting light while the shadows of the night gathered in the darkening forest. A vast silence enveloped the small hunched figure as he drew the blanket closer, the blanket that Haru had woven for him in the first month of his life. But there was no Haru, no warmth, only nothingness and the nagging question in Tijo's mind: *What will happen to me?*

CHAPTER 1

The Darkness

A fine rain scratched the night. It had been strange for Hold On since the fire. The stallion could feel. He could smell. He could hear. But he could not see. He lived in a shadow world of confusing shades of blacks and grays. The stars above were invisible no matter what the weather. However, his remaining senses were becoming sharper, and he smelled the rain before it came.

He found himself thinking longingly of the comforts he had disdained for so long — the comforts of the stall where hay and water were brought each day, where grooms might curry his coat, rub his joints and his sore tendons so tenderly. Yet it was foolish to think of the old ways now. He might be blind, but he was wild. They had escaped and left the Old

World of men behind. They were in the New World now. Hold On shook his head as if to rid himself of these torturous thoughts, as though a swarm of flies were buzzing through his mind. He had been a captive then, a tool for humans. He refused to become a traitor to freedom, to wildness.

In his mind's eye, there was the dim flicker of the young filly Estrella.

It was Estrella who had led Hold On and the other horses away from that terrible world of men. Her dam, Perlina, had died, torn apart by a shark when they were cast overboard by the Ibers. But the other horses had survived, and despite having never set hoof to earth until that beach, Estrella had really been born wild. Hold On, however, had been born in the old country, shod by the blacksmith when he was a few months old.

How odd it was that it had been Estrella who first showed him how to forget the ways of men, forget the gaits he had been taught, the bridle and bit that had been shoved in his mouth. How to unlearn all that and discover what it meant to run free. Had she died in the canyon fire? Would he ever see her again? A wave of despair rose within him.

Hold On and the first herd had been led into that canyon by the treacherous stallion Pego, when a fire had broken out. The flames had singed Hold On's mane and burned his tail until it was just a charred stub. It was the fire that had blinded him. He had no idea if Estrella and the rest of the first herd had perished. Somehow he had escaped. He had been blinded, his lungs seared, but he was alive.

He squinted and looked for that last pale layer of the night, the skin of the night before the pink flesh of the new day. It was still dark, too dark, but was there a smudge in the sky? Was it the moon? Could he borrow just a bit of moonlight to find a place to sleep? He wanted to capture it behind his eyelids, save it, cosset it, polish it, and in that way he might once again find his old friends.

He would need all his senses to find them, but especially his eyes. He knew the tracks of each horse. Angela and Corazón touched down lightly, as if a ghost of their old gaits hovered just beneath their hoofprints in the earth. Grullo, the heaviest, had a deep track, whereas Estrella's hooves seemed to barely touch the earth when she galloped. For Estrella had never been shod, never worn a saddle, never been broken. There was a remarkable purity that surrounded her like the starry dust of an ancient night.

He wanted to find them all. He was lonely in this dark and empty new world.

Not half a league away in the softly drizzling rain, the boy began to dig a grave. The earth was soft, so the digging went quickly. He wrapped the frail body of Haru in the thin antelope skin he had brought for this purpose, and gently laid her down on her back with a stone propped under her head. That way, she could watch the stars even when the dirt was piled on, for the eyes of the dead could see through earth into the next world, the world of Otang. In addition to the antelope hide, he had brought a shiny black piece of obsidian and placed it in her mouth. The stone would turn to honey and nourish her as she traveled the trail. It was all the food she would need.

It did not take him long to finish burying her. He took the pipe and stuffed in the shredded cedar bark he had brought. Relighting the pipe took time because the bark was damp and he couldn't let his mouth touch it, for it was Haru's pipe, and to properly send her off, there must be the mark of her lips only on the pipe stem. So he blew into the bowl of the pipe long enough to rekindle the ashes. Then he lifted the pipe into the air, turning to the north, and began to recite the first verses of the mourning song:

Shadow of the wind,
Flash of the firefly,
Vapor of breath when the night is cold,
Such is your life on earth.

But comes the everlasting
In the lap of mother sky,
Go you on the way to Otang.

He recited this song four times: first to the north, then to the east, then to the south, and finally to the west. The wind shifted suddenly, blowing the smoke and the words back into his face, but he continued singing until all the cedar in the pipe had burned.

CHAPTER 2

A Dream Snatched

Hold On had finally fallen into a dreamless sleep, a dark void with no flames, no singed manes, when the scent of smoke jolted him awake. *Fire!* He began to tremble so hard, he thought his legs might buckle. The blackness was still thick. He took a step forward and bumped into the trunk of the piñon tree. He backed away and began to walk slowly in circles. He heard a dry rapid clatter. *Snake!* he thought, the bad snake whose bite was poisonous. He reared slightly and jumped aside only to knock his hindquarters against another tree. But now there was something worse than the clatter snake. Another scent. That of a human. He froze and opened his eyes wide and stared into the emptiness.

When Tijo was finished, he tucked the pipe away, pulled the thick sheep hide around his shoulders, and sat down to think. Where should he go? Back to the clan? Without Haru he would become *omo*, not cast out like a malformed baby but turned into a living ghost. No one would speak to him. No one would share food with him. At first, they would avert their eyes or pretend not to see him, and finally they would actually look right through him as if he were transparent. He would become air and then he would finally die.

A person normally became *omo* as punishment for some transgression — not a serious crime like murder but after violating some code of behavior. The shunning would commence in a small way, then it was like a contagion. Other people would join in, or else it might suggest the misbehavior was acceptable, which would threaten the integrity of the band. Tijo looked down at his crooked leg. It was enough to threaten the sturdiness of the band. No parent would want their daughter to become friends with Tijo. Marriage would be forbidden.

That had always been clear. For as long as he could remember, he'd been kept separate from other children. He could not play their games or learn to hunt alongside them. Haru had been his only playmate and his only teacher. He knew practically nothing of the communal life of the band. He and Haru lived always a short distance away from them. They made their own cooking fires. Dug their own latrine. Stood apart at the ceremonies. That had been his life, and now if he returned, it would be worse.

He could not go back to the band. It would be an insult to Haru. If Haru sat in the lap of the Spirit Mother at the end of the spirit trail, did she want to look down and see the boy she had raised for eleven years treated so miserably? It would make her cry. Tears from the spirit world caused bad things to happen — drought, sickness, famine — even tears shed for a lame boy. He got up to stretch. If the people of the band wanted a ghost, they would have one.

The ground was still damp and he noticed the prints of an animal he did not recognize. He crouched down and ran his hand over the impression in the mud. The creature had no toes. The hoof, or whatever this strange shape was called, was not cloven and it was big and sank deep into the mud like that of the big-horned mountain sheep. What could it be? Tijo recalled how Haru's nose had twitched just before she died. He bent down and picked up the faintest trace of a scent he had never known. *Haru had smelled this creature!*

The tracks were pronounced and easy to follow, but they seemed to be going in circles, as if the creature was lost.

The rain finally began to taper off. Mist rose from the thinly wooded stand of piñon and birch trees. Tijo halted abruptly and stared in disbelief. Beneath a piñon tree stood the most immense creature he had ever seen. It was shivering and at intervals its entire hide appeared to flinch. Its pointed ears were laid back. Tijo approached quietly, but the creature jerked its head around and snorted. Its odor was different from the oily one of sheep or the meaty one of mountain lions, and there was a more powerful overlying smell of charred hair or fur. His coat was a silvery gray but streaked with smoky marks. This creature had passed through a fire, one of the canyon fires that sometimes ignited at this time of year. It turned its head toward Tijo and peeled back its lips in a strange manner.

Tijo could tell that the creature was frightened. Frightened and lost. As the mist swirled about, it appeared like a specter before the dawn. *And I believed I was the ghost here,* Tijo thought. This animal truly looked as if it had fallen off the trail to Otang. It seemed lost between two worlds. The mist billowed around them more thickly. The light of the moon gave this place an eerie luminosity. Tijo felt as if he were standing nowhere but everywhere, a place that was suspended in a fold between air and water, cloud and earth. A strong gust suddenly rustled the trees, and a swarm of clouds stampeded across the moon as utter blackness descended. When it cleared off, the creature had vanished. *I must have dreamed it,* Tijo thought, and blinked. A dream snatcher must have come and ripped the cloth of his sleep. It could happen. Such a wind could tear the strongest filaments of a spider's web. His vision of the creature could not have been real. *Creatures like that appear only in dreams.*

CHAPTER 3

The Light of the Dark, Dark of the Light

Estrella nibbled at the bluff grass and thought of Hold On. Even though eight other horses grazed nearby, the haunting loneliness had not lessened since they had emerged from the fiery canyon almost four days before. If anything, it had grown worse. It was as if there were a hole in her world, in her body. And now that hole was filled only with longing. Her dreams were tortured by images of Hold On that would not dissipate. He had been by her side the whole time in the canyon. In fact, for a few brief minutes, he had been ahead of her. The stallion's tail had ignited and flared out like a torch and then it had just burned off.

"Your tail! Your tail!" she had whinnied.

"Never mind my tail. Just keep running!" He had begun to

cough. They all had been coughing. However, nothing could stop the powerful old stallion. He kept galloping at full speed. Next she remembered hearing a loud thud. He had stumbled. Shortly after that, she had felt the wetness on her hooves and knew that a creek was trickling from what had appeared to be a solid rock wall. She'd realized there might be a way out, an escape. That's when she spotted the tiny horselike figure glowing in the gauzy light. It had turned and beckoned with its head, as if to say, *This way! This way!* She had followed and had not even noticed that Hold On was not with them until they were out of the canyon. How could he have disappeared so quickly? Had he hurt a leg? Or had the rampaging flames of the fire simply caught up and swallowed him?

Estrella and the herd had moved only a few leagues since leaving the fiery canyon. The winds had been gusty, and every once in a while, there came a familiar scent she thought might belong to Hold On. But none of the others believed her. Was it even real? It seemed that her sense of smell had been shredded by the smoke and ash. She could not trust it. She felt as if she were being pulled in so many different and often conflicting directions. Sometimes she thought she picked up the fragrance of the sweet grass that the first horse seemed to be leading her toward, but now it was all tangled up.

She missed Hold On more desperately each day. He was the largest horse of the herd, and she loved the sound

of the pounding heart in his huge chest when they galloped side by side. She loved the smell of the sweat flying off
his withers. She missed standing next to him beneath a
starry sky and hearing him speak of what he called meadow
wisdom — all the pungent secrets that men could never teach
them or know that they knew.

She knew the herd expected her to lead them, lead them to
the sweet grass that would allow them to survive the harsh
winter. She felt their eyes looking at her now, especially Corazón
and Angela, who watched her with the most vigilance. The
two old mares were the last to give up their old ways, who had
been most attached to their masters. Estrella found it hard to
understand how any horse could feel affection for those Iber
men who had forced their heads into bridles, put bits in their
mouths, and used whips to urge them on.

She recognized the sound of Corazón's hooves as the mare
approached. She was a cream-colored horse with a scattering of
dark gray spots. Now the spots did not stand out so much, as
her entire coat was smudged with ash from the fire.

"Dear," she began. "We know you are mourning."

Estrella snapped her head about. "Don't say *mourn*. He
might not be dead. Hold On might still be alive, just lost." She
walked away before she could see the mares' stunned reactions.

Angela watched Estrella go, then whispered to Corazón,
"She turned on you just like that? How rude."

"Let her be, Angela. We have to give her time."

"But time is what we might be short on, Corazón. You felt that chill in the air last night. Winter's coming. We need to get to good grazing land."

"Good grazing land will all be under snow by winter. It won't matter. If we grow weak from hunger, if we go slow, it will be either the winter or the men who will catch us."

Bobtail, a bright bay stallion, trotted up to the two mares. "Well, what shall we do? Turn south? Go back to where we've been? To the Iber, to the Chitzen?" Corazón shuddered. They once had longed for their old masters, but not now, not when they saw what these humans were capable of in this new world with their thirst for gold and power.

They all swung their heads toward Estrella. They wanted her back the way she had been. The filly who was clever beyond her years and held the map of the stars in her head. The one who'd broken into a joyous gallop the first time her hooves had touched land and reminded them what it meant to be free.

Later that day, it began to rain. The horses gathered in a grove of cottonwoods near a pond for shelter, but even as they huddled side by side, they barely uttered a word. They hardly exchanged glances. The tension within the herd had grown so thick, it felt heavier than a saddle.

When the rain finally stopped and the reflections of the evening stars trembled on the surface of the pond, Estrella walked to the edge of the water and studied them, wondering where that tiny starry horse could have gone.

In the most stressful moments, the tiny horse had always emerged. When they had been captured in the City of the Gods and the Ibers tried to break her, hobbling her legs and forcing a bit into her mouth, she had fought them, and all the while that tiny horse had flickered in her mind. Then it had appeared to her as a carved figure, sprinting across the rock face of a cliff.

It was this tiny horse that had led them out of the flames. She yearned for him and yearned for Hold On as well. Together they were the polestars of her mind.

But the memory of the little horse was melting away, fading. *I shall be left with nothing!* How could she be expected to lead the herd on her own?

Winter would be coming. They needed good grass to graze on. They had to fatten themselves up. The grass here was thin and dry, and no matter how much they grazed they still felt empty. Witch grass, she heard Corazón and Angela call it. For it tricked you so that at first you felt full but shortly there came a gnawing hunger. The more one ate, the hungrier one felt.

There were moments when a sudden shift of wind brought a hint of Hold On's familiar scent, but then it vanished within a second, as if the wind were taunting her with her memories of the old stallion. The scent was like the odd tricks of light that happened in this open barren country, creating eerie images that sometimes loomed up on the horizon and looked quite real, but then as one came closer, the pictures disintegrated into nothing. Most often the illusion was an image of water — a lake suddenly appearing in the distance, or the sharp towering shapes that looked as solid as rock yet trembled slightly. The land swept ahead endlessly. She could see mountains etched on the distant horizon. She looked at the rest of the herd. They seemed tiny in this vastness, as tiny as the specks of stars in the enormousness of the night.

Corazón neighed softly. "She won't go on until, well, until . . ."

"Hold On." Angela said the name of the stallion. "Just say it, Corazón. You know that's why the filly can't let go."

Corazón sighed. "She can't grieve forever. It's time to move on."

Their bellies and their minds, their imaginations, were on the brink of starvation, and soon it would be winter. "Perhaps we should let the men find us. They might've built warm stables," Corazón said, a wistful note in her voice.

Then Angela truly surprised Corazón. She whipped her head around and looked at her old friend steadily. "I don't want to go back, Corazón. I don't ever want to go back to the world of men. I know it might sound silly. I never would have believed I would be saying such a thing. But we are not just free, Corazón."

"What do you mean?"

"Free just means free of humans, free of shoes, free of saddles, free of bridles and bits and gaits that cling to our hooves like cobwebs. No, we are much more."

"Bless my withers, what are we, then?"

"We are wild!" Angela whispered the word as if it were a dangerous secret.

"Does that mean we can never ever go back to our master?" Corazón asked.

"I don't think they would take us," Angela said. She pinned back her ears and began to tremble. "We are on our own."

And soon, thought Estrella, *they will be starving. And it will be my fault.* Estrella had in fact been half listening to the old horses. She looked over at the two elderly mares. They had been the last ones to give up their gaits, to relinquish all the artifices that the Ibers had inflicted upon them. They had come a long way, and yet now they seemed on the brink of going back. Estrella shut her eyes. It was unbearable to watch. It was she who had failed, not the mares. She had led them to this point. Angela was right. There was a difference between being free and being wild. She remembered Hold On talking about being owned, that it was an unnatural condition, that even when the bit wasn't in your mouth, it always seemed to be there. How had he said it? "The shape hovers in your mouth. The taste of metal is never really gone. It's as if the bit is in your brain, and you know that sooner or later it will be coming."

Estrella wanted more than anything to find Hold On, but what was the cost? Did it mean betraying the other horses? Was she actually leading the first herd back to their shoes? To the shape that Hold On had told her hovers in your mouth?

Estrella had been born on that ship, yet no one had broken her. They had tried when they captured her at the City of the Gods, but she had escaped. Her freedom had been a bit of luck combined with a fierce will. Angela was right. Being free was just getting loose from something that had bound you, while being wild . . . that was very different. Wild meant being true to your nature, honoring what you were meant to be and not what you had been forced into being by men. Being wild meant being whole and not broken. Being wild — that was her heritage. It was her nature and it was her destiny. *I am wild.* And she squeezed her eyes shut trying to conjure the image of that first tiny wild horse. Still it would not come. There was only darkness.

CHAPTER 4
Big Dog

For Tijo, there had been no dream snatcher. The creature was real and had been easy for him to track. His immense hooves, four times the size of a dog's paws and twice or three times the size of the big-horned sheep's, left distinct prints in the ground after the rainstorm. And then there were its droppings. Huge round lumps left in piles like no scat the boy had ever seen. For three days now, he had been tracking the animal as soundlessly as he could. Tijo always attempted to stay downwind so the creature would not catch his scent. But sometimes it was impossible and he would hear the creature pant nervously or emit a high-pitched sound like no bark he had ever heard. For indeed Tijo had begun to think of him as an enormous dog — Big Dog.

Tijo had eaten almost all the jerky in his pack, and his stomach growled softly. Big Dog heard it and shot off, nearly crashing into a tree. So although he could hear and smell, there was something wrong with his sight. Tijo had suspected this early on, for Big Dog often ambled in circles endlessly over a rather small area.

Was he frightened because he had never seen a creature like Tijo? Or perhaps he had seen one and was fearful that the boy was hunting him. How could Tijo tell him that he was not a predator and that he would never in a million moons think of Big Dog as prey? Never! *Patient. You must be patient!* He could hear Haru's voice counseling him.

If Tijo had learned anything from his years of lameness, it was patience. He remembered Haru saying to him, "You are as good as any other boy your age and a lot smarter. You just have to go slower. You must learn to be patient. Patience can be like a muscle and make you stronger. Help you see things more clearly."

Bobtail stomped his hoof and snorted. "Winter is coming. We cannot delay. We have to move. Move, Estrella. Now!" The chestnut stallion's ears were pinned back, his dark eyes flashing.

Estrella felt a flicker of unease but refused to look away.

"Am I the only one who caught Hold On's scent? I swear I smelled him." She turned to Grullo, the dun-colored stallion. He was a steady fellow. Intelligent, with keen sensibilities. Never spooked and slow to judge. "Grullo, you must have caught the scent. Didn't you?"

He shook his head wearily. "I did not, Estrella."

"And if he did," Bobtail continued, "what would that mean?"

Grullo looked sharply at Bobtail. "It would mean a great deal, Bobtail."

Estrella was stunned. "What does it mean? It means Hold On is near and we must search for him. Are you doubting that I picked up his scent?"

"No," Grullo answered gently. "But sometimes we can be misled. Estrella, I hear you in your dreams calling out for him. Your head is full of Hold On. We understand that. You were so close. He was like a sire to you. But even so . . ."

"What Grullo is trying to say," Corazón continued for him, "is that you are being obstinate."

"I agree," Bobtail snorted.

The words were harsh ones, and Estrella flinched.

"Estrella," Sky the colt said in a tentative voice, "you can't look for Hold On forever. The grass will grow thinner. We're already going to sleep hungry. We're running out of time."

No! Estrella wanted to scream. "Are you saying I am fooling myself? Did not one of you catch his scent?"

"I thought perhaps I did, though only for such a flicker of a moment," Angela said. "But still."

"But still what?" Estrella demanded.

Now Arriero, a dark bay stallion, stepped forward. "But still we do not have time for wild chases. The grass here is no good. It is worse than no good. We feel hungrier every time we eat it."

"Witch grass," muttered Corazón.

"Perhaps," Grullo said, "we can give it one or two more days. But that is it, Estrella. Then we must head north, for that is where you said we shall find the sweet grass."

"No!" Bobtail whinnied shrilly. "If Estrella wants to stay, that's her choice. But the rest of us are leaving."

The two colts, Verdad and Sky, exchanged nervous glances. Sky stepped hesitantly forward. He had one dark eye and one blue eye, and both were full of fear. "Are . . . are you saying, Bobtail, we should split the herd?"

"That is exactly what he is saying," Arriero snorted.

A silence enveloped the herd.

Estrella looked at each of the horses. There were bonds among them that simply could not be broken. That's what being a herd meant. They needed one another. But Hold On needed them, too. How could she convince them not to give up hope?

"I will not risk splitting the herd. If you insist upon going, I shall go. Each of us is valuable. Each of us is needed. But we also need Hold On. And he's out there, counting on us to help him. So can we compromise? Let us stay just one day and then we can move on, I promise."

She felt a thaw in their resistance. Corazón and Angela shifted uneasily, suddenly unwilling to meet Estrella's eyes. Sky stared into the distance, as if he was imagining what it would feel like to be out there on his own, herdless.

After a long moment, Bobtail spoke. "Hold On never gave up on us when we were scared, when we didn't believe we had the strength to live apart from men." Bobtail's eyes had a faraway look, as if he was recalling that night. He sighed. "And so I believe that we should wait one more day and hope to pick up the stallion's track."

Estrella nodded her head. "Thank you, Bobtail. Thank you." She could not help but notice that the hoof that had been stomping so furiously a short time before was now resting quietly on the ground.

Tijo had been patient and kept creeping a little closer to Big Dog. Now they were in a thin stand of trees with little between them but the shivers of the leaves on the branches. Tijo couldn't have been more than five strides from the mysterious creature.

He crouched behind a boulder, when something startled Big Dog. He reared and shied, bumping into a tree before falling to his knees. Cursing his lame leg, Tijo ran as fast as he could to where Big Dog was trying to scramble to his feet. He appeared ready to bolt at any second, but there was another tree dead ahead. Taking care to avoid flying hooves, Tijo reached out. Hold On flinched at the boy's first touch, but did not bolt when Tijo began rubbing the creature in circles just beneath the withers. Though he did not have withers himself, he recalled Haru rubbing the base of his neck after some boys jumped on him, trying to beat him, when he was very young.

"You're like me! Alone. So alone," Tijo whispered.

The boy's touch was light. He was speaking softly in a language the stallion did not understand.

As he leaned over Hold On, the boy realized that the creature's wide staring eyes saw nothing.

"You are blind. Fire has blinded you." The creature had the smell of a grass eater and his blunt teeth were harmless. "And you are thirsty. I can take you to water.

"Come! Come." But what should Tijo call him? There was no name for such a creature in his language. "Come, Big Dog," he said finally, unable to think of anything else.

Hold On's fear settled into confusion. The boy's touch was welcoming. He could feel the warm blood beneath the skin of his fingertips. He felt the boy's hand slide down to stroke his shoulders. A calmness began to steal through him. The boy was saying something very softly but with a gentle urgency. *He wants me to stand. He fears that I have injured my legs when, instead, I had just given up.* And so the old stallion shoved his front legs forward, and with Tijo murmuring encouragement, Hold On wiggled his hindquarters and stood up again. He sensed that this person was small, just a boy.

"Ah! You stand tall like the fine Big Dog you are. Now follow me, Big Dog, and I shall take you to grass."

Hold On was amazed. The boy did not try to put a bridle on him or a rope around his neck. He merely began to walk a few paces ahead. And Hold On followed. Followed the scent that was the boy. It was a complicated scent. There was the fragrance of cedar, a slightly salty odor, and another more elusive scent, as if he had been close to something that had died recently. With this scent came the smell of sorrow, of sorrow mixed with loneliness. Or perhaps aloneness. The boy had not been around other humans very often. *We are alike,* Hold On thought as he followed the boy. *Both separated from our herd.*

Tijo took Hold On across the stream to where a fine patch of the silver sage called winterfat grew. "Here you are," the boy said softly, and picked up a bunch of the stiff grass. Big Dog sniffed it, then took a tentative bite. "Same color as your coat — or at least where the smoke didn't smudge it." The unsoiled patches reminded Tijo of the dappled light in early winter when the sun still seemed to want to stay out longer despite the shortening of the days. Tijo had already decided he was going to wash Big Dog and make his coat bright and silvery again. But first he would do something for his eyes. He noticed as the night thinned that Big Dog began tossing his head about as if looking toward the sky.

"What do you look for? What do you feel?" Tijo asked. He wondered if perhaps this creature was like Haru, but instead of smelling weather, Big Dog could smell light, even though he could not see it.

Tijo was short and Hold On was tall. But now he wanted to look straight into those dark sightless eyes. There was a boulder nearby.

"Come, Big Dog." The creature seemed to understand. Tijo scrambled up on the rock without touching Hold On's face and peered deeply into his eyes. It was like looking into a starless night. He could see that they wept almost constantly and the eyelids were very swollen. Tijo remembered that when he was very young and something had blown in his eyes, Haru had made a paste from the sap of a broadleaf plant called old man's cane. He would find it and milk it, then mix it with the sap from the medicine tree, the piñon tree.

But for the remainder of this night, he would make sure

that Big Dog drank and ate the silver sage. Perhaps he had followed Haru for another reason beyond that of making sure she did not die alone.

Hold On stood patiently by a creek with his eyes squeezed shut while the boy climbed up on a log and applied the paste. This was the third time he had treated his eyes. It seemed to Tijo that not only was the puffiness decreasing but he could almost feel a pulse beneath the eyelids, as if the creature's eyes were scanning some half-lit landscape.

"What are you seeing, Old Fellow?" Hold On gave a muffled snort. How could the boy ever understand that he belonged to a herd? They were comprehending more of each other's odd language every day. That was why the boy now addressed him as Old Fellow rather than Big Dog. Tijo sensed that Hold On did not like being called that name.

Hold On was seeing something that was very hard to explain even if he and the boy had shared a language. The very image that had eluded Estrella twinkled beneath his eyelids. Could it be the constellation, the winged stallion for which Pego had been named? But no, this horse had no wings and it was very small. It did not stand still in the sky but was moving very fast, much more swiftly than the measured pace of the transit of the stars across the sky. Hold On could almost feel the vapor of the tiny horse's breath each time it had turned to beckon him. This must be the same tiny horse that Estrella had pointed to that day, the one that had glistened in the crystal-studded rock face. The first horse had returned for him.

But would the tiny horse lead him back to his herd? This boy had done much for him, but Hold On belonged with his herd, and the boy belonged with his people. Yet Hold On realized he had never known a human quite like this boy. They had seemed to enter each other's heads, or was it each other's dreams, for it was all still darkness for Hold On, a long dark tunnel into an endless night. Although the tunnel was not so lonely now, and the darkness seemed to be thinning into a feeble dawn.

"What's that, Old Fellow?" For Tijo could tell that the creature, though standing still, had wandered far off into his own private shadowland. Might he be able to help Old Fellow navigate through that shadowland? Tijo wondered. But winter would come and then who would help him? To be alone when the cold winds peeled off the mountains to the north would mean certain death. They were called wolf storms because their front edges were like fangs of ice and could tear apart a dozen lodges in a short time. The best refuges were cliff dwellings. But how would Old Fellow find a cliff dwelling without Tijo? And how would Tijo be able to move through heavy snow and ice? Was it possible that he and Old Fellow might be able to help each other survive the savage winter? They were an unlikely pair. But who else was there? He had already decided that returning to his village was impossible. When the aging chief died, the healer would undoubtedly take over. A brutal, ruthless man who had always been jealous of Haru, and had hastened her death with the tainted cup.

As he rubbed Old Fellow's ears, he muttered to himself, "All we have is each other, Old Fellow. Just each other, and here we are on the rim of winter." He felt a chill pass through him as if one of those icy fangs of the wolf storms had reached out and traced its tip down his spine. "Just each other," he said again, and Hold On's ears seemed to pivot about as he ducked his head, burying his muzzle in the warmth of Tijo's armpit.

CHAPTER 5

A Horse Named Pego

Pego's huge heart was pounding in his chest as he stretched into a full gallop across the hard-packed land, fueled by an engulfing anger. He couldn't believe his herd had turned on him, just because he had better things to do than tend to a sick mare. Yes, she'd been carrying his colt, but that didn't mean Pego had to abandon all his plans.

But his herd hadn't seen it that way. They'd looked at him with cold horror. Even Azul, his own filly! She wanted to lead. Pego saw it in her eyes. He had to admit that in a certain way Azul was just like him, but the feeling in his heaving chest was nothing close to pride.

He stopped now on a rise. He had gone quite a distance since he left the others three days before. One could make good time traveling alone. It was dawn, and as the sun climbed into the sky, pale bands of light began to spread on the horizon. A wind stirred the grass. The possibilities seemed endless in such a land. It could all be his. He would find a new mare. A new herd to lead.

A familiar scent wound through the air. Pego stiffened. Then a narrow yellow face with tilting green eyes slipped out from a burrow.

"And so we meet again, old friend."

"What do you want?" Pego snapped.

Coyote cocked his head to the side and surveyed Pego. "Azul and Lourdes were fools. The blood of the *Pura Raza* runs in their veins and yet they turn squeamish! Shocking. You know what the color of their livers are? Yellow — yellow as my coat. Yellow as the lily flowers."

"Yes, yes, I suppose you are right," Pego said, warming to Coyote's voice and feeling his own outrage at those horses boil up anew.

"I know it's hard on you. I understand," Coyote said, his voice thick with empathy.

"I had wanted to start a herd. My own herd."

"And you shall! How would you like to lead a herd of six hundred horses?"

Pego tossed his head with a snort. "That is impossible. Where will I find six hundred horses?"

"El Miedo," Coyote said, savoring the word.

"El Miedo!" Pego had heard of that great Iber. Though he had never seen him, he could picture him: a man even larger and stronger than the Seeker, with regal bearing and ambition in his face.

"You know him, Pego?"

"Of course. El Miedo. His name means the One Who Is Feared."

"And do you know who feared him the most? The Seeker. The very man who left you to die in this new world."

"You are right!" Pego said with an indignant toss of his head.

"I know what you're thinking." Coyote slithered up to the stallion and gave him a friendly nudge with his muzzle on his hocks. "We have become *socios*, associates, partners, so to speak."

The coyote had slipped into Pego's dreams. Yearn, yearn deeply enough for anything and Coyote will come. But Pego did not understand this completely. He did not realize that the yearning was like an open wound that, once licked by Coyote, could fester.

"El Miedo shall not call you Pego," Coyote said.

Pego's ears flattened. "But that is my name. That was what my first master, Don Arturo, named me. He named me for the constellation, the sky horse Pegasus. I am a *Pura Raza*."

Coyote shook his head in mild disgust. "He will have a better name for you. El Noble."

"The Noble One?" Pego's ears suddenly pricked forward. He peeled back his lips as if to smell the name.

"Yes, I think it suits. Don't you?" Coyote asked.

"Yes . . . Yes, of course." The rising bands of color had stretched over the entire sky. Pego tipped his head up and basked in the reflected glory of the dawn. The sun began to warm his face. He felt anointed, blessed, as if a crown had been placed on his head.

And so the pair set off together, and spent two days traveling in a southerly direction. On the morning of the third day, they caught the scent. It burst upon the landscape like a suddenly blooming flower — the sweet dung scent of six hundred horses and two score of mules and donkeys.

Pego broke into a weary trot.

"Slow down!" Coyote yipped.

"What? Why? You said he is expecting me. In his dreams he had visions of such a horse as I. El Noble."

"You do not look noble right now."

"I don't?"

"There's a slow stream over there. Take a look at yourself."

Pego glared at Coyote, then tossed his head and approached

the stream warily. He peered at his reflection. His almost black coat was dusty and in places encrusted with the rime of dried sweat. His mane and tail were strung with burrs. He looked as shabby as any field horse.

"Take a bath!" Coyote urged. Pego entered the stream and walked to where a deep pool formed. He hunkered down in it for several minutes, then emerged, shaking the water out of his long mane.

"So now we can go," Pego said, twitching to shake the water out of his coat.

"Not quite yet," Coyote replied. "There is still work to be done."

"What work?"

Once again, Coyote shook his head in a gesture of disgust and his green eyes seemed to slide around. "You have lost your gaits."

Pego stood erect. His neck arched in indignation. "What are you talking about?

"I saw you trying a *paso fino* the other day. You looked like a savage. El Miedo won't have use for a warhorse that moves like a mule. I suggest you start practicing." The *paso fino* was an elegant four-beat gait somewhere between a walk and a canter and was performed on a slant.

"But what if El Miedo moves the herd?"

"El Miedo is not moving fast, believe me. He has five

hundred men, six hundred horses, fourscore or more carts. We have time. Now start practicing! Let's begin with the *paso fino*."

They practiced for an entire morning — all the gaits that well-bred horses were trained to perform with *brio*. That was the term the Iber used to describe the crisp vigor, controlled energy, and, most important, the willingness to serve a rider. It was all to serve the rider. For these were animals in thrall to humans every moment of their lives, even when they were bred. The proper mate was selected by humans in the hopes of producing another *Pura Raza* that could carry on the bloodlines of the Jennet, the Barbs, those species that began in the deserts of Arabia, the wellspring of the most noble horses in the world. God's horses!

As the sun crossed over into the western sky, Pego's impatience grew. "When? When can we go?"

Coyote sighed in exasperation. How truly unimaginative this horse was! With studied patience he began to explain. "When you go, it shall be dark, pitch-black except for the moon and the stars. The constellation for which you were named shall ride high in the sky. Its light will bless you. You will gleam in the darkness, illuminated by the stars like the god you were born to be." Coyote paused. "Do you now understand?"

"I understand, compadre," Pego replied solemnly.

"Good. Now back to practice. I want to see that *andadura* once more."

Coyote watched the moon climb over the horizon.

"Not yet. Not yet," he whispered. He wanted it perfectly positioned, low in the sky but with the first stars breaking out just above. "Soon . . . soon . . . you'll hear me howl, then step out."

They were in a grove of piñon trees not far from El Miedo's encampment. El Miedo was sleeping in his tent. The first howl of Coyote wound through his dreams. The second howl woke him. He heard the horses in the nearby corral stirring. Something was coming. The braying of mules twined through the chill air of the night. He pulled on his boots and grabbed his blade, the Crusader dagger from Toledo, where the finest blacksmiths in the world forged the steel in their fires. The horses were whinnying nervously. He heard some guards mumbling, "*Un sueño negro, sueño oscuro*." A dark dream.

The words resonated in his head. How would they know what his dreams had been these last restless nights? The dream shadows that streamed through his sleep. Then his eyes opened. It was here. *El caballo de destino*, destiny's horse. El Noble.

The horse loomed up against the rising moon. Its dark coat caught the chips of starlight like diamonds in the night. The stallion leaned into the wind as he pranced in a *paso de aire*, air steps in which he appeared suspended against the moon while performing a four-beat ambling gait

"El Noble! He is here at last!" El Miedo whispered. He felt his blood stir, and knew that with this horse his destiny was assured.

CHAPTER 6

"Hold On! That Is Your Name!"

Tijo and Old Fellow's days fell into a comfortable pattern. Tijo would lead the stallion by walking ahead of him. The only time he touched him was to put the salve on his eyes. He thought it was helping, but he couldn't be sure. The swelling had certainly gone down. But then again, having never seen such a creature as Old Fellow, Tijo was not sure what his eyes were supposed to look like. However, there was one thing of which Tijo was certain. The creature could almost see with his ears. His hearing was extraordinary. He would swing his head suddenly toward the sizzling noise of a grasshopper and immediately head for that clump of grass without Tijo leading him. At night he picked up the clicking sounds of the desert bats weaving through the darkness, and sometimes he would make a noise to orient himself, like a bat. On these occasions he would stop and whinny softly in the direction of a rock or a cliff, to see if an echo came back.

Tijo loved to watch Old Fellow's ears. He had never seen a creature whose ears could move so independently of each other. They twitched every which way as he collected the sounds of a moment: the burred trills of chickadees, then the swooping notes of a blue-throated sparrow and the soft shivering song of a plover all laced through the sunlight.

For Old Fellow, it was as if there were sound pictures scribbled on the wind. But soon Tijo began to suspect that it was not just sound or scent that filled the sightless world of the creature but in fact he was becoming more sensitive to light. Old Fellow still stumbled, perhaps not quite as often, but Tijo sensed that his vision was improving.

On the third day, Tijo led Old Fellow to the low flat sand banks of a shallow meandering creek that ribboned through great swaths of white sage. The tumbling water of the creek danced with spangled glints of sunlight. It was a beautiful day. Old Fellow's ears flicked this way and that as he listened to the sound of the creek.

But now Tijo noticed a ghost of movement beneath Old Fellow's eyelids. Was it the glints of sun bouncing off the creek's rippled surface?

Hold On took a step closer to the water's edge. Tijo's heart quickened. The sand here was called the cleaning sand. This was a creek where people often bathed or brought the fleece of their sheep to wash. Would Old Fellow let Tijo wash him? He wanted to scrub the smoke and ash that so darkened what he felt was a beautiful coat.

Tijo waded in deeper ahead and then turned around. "Come! Come along," he coaxed. Hold On took another step. The water swirled around his hocks, and some of the filth of the fire turned the curling foam dark as it ran downstream. Tijo dared to crouch down and, cupping his hands, scooped up some of the fine white sand from the creek bottom.

He began to gently rub the wet sand up from Old Fellow's hooves to his hocks. "There you are!" he said as he saw the hair lighten. Old Fellow remained calm. He seemed to enjoy the feel of the boy's hands rubbing the sand against his coat. Tijo's eyes widened. It looked like a new horse was emerging out of the sooty hide. He was a silvery gray with darker spots, like a night sky with the moon and stars scudding behind pale clouds.

The water was now up to the boy's waist and he could not quite reach to the stallion's withers. He so wanted to see this "new" creature all clean and glowing. Tijo felt his own feet leave the bottom as the current lifted him up. He was treading water now beside Old Fellow's shoulders. But it was hard to tread water and scrub. The charred ends of Old Fellow's mane had broken off days before, but there were still dark streaks. He wondered if Old Fellow would notice if he held on to a hank of the mane. Would it hurt him? For if he could just hold on, he could steady himself in the water better and have one hand free for scrubbing. They were coming to the deepest part of the creek. What would happen if it was too deep for Old Fellow? Could this creature swim?

Tijo pressed his face close to Old Fellow's ear. "Old Fellow, my friend, may I hold on?" Old Fellow turned his head toward the boy. For the first time, his eyelids were entirely open. He looked deep into the boy's eyes. "May I hold on?" Tijo repeated.

The water stirred as the creature's withers flinched and he gave a soft whinny, a sound unlike any that Tijo had ever heard. The horse kept his nearly sightless gaze on Tijo. His ears, which had been soft and relaxed, now pricked forward as if listening intently, and he whinnied a second time as if to say, *Say again, say again, please?*

"Hold On! Hold On! That is your name!"

He grabbed the soot-streaked mane as Hold On's hooves left the creek bed and suddenly he was floating. The powerful legs began to churn the water. "Hold On! I am holding on!" Tijo shouted joyously into the clear blue dome of the sky. Hold On rolled his body slightly to one side, and Tijo felt himself float up above his back. His legs straddled Hold

On's barrel. It felt more like flying than swimming. The big muscles of Hold On's shoulders worked rhythmically as they powered down the center of the creek. Tijo leaned close to his withers.

He was not sure how long they had been swimming, but soon Tijo felt Hold On's hooves striking the creek bed again. Tijo slid back toward his rump, still grasping his mane as Hold On heaved himself from the water up the steep bank. Then the stallion began to shake the water from his body. Tijo gripped with his knees as hard as he could to keep astride.

Hold On felt the pressure of the boy's knees. One leg seemed to grip tighter than the other and was not quite as strong, but he soon grew accustomed to it. What he was not accustomed to was the boy's weight. Never in all his years of service to the Ibers had anyone felt so light on his back.

There was no bit, no bridle, no spurs, and yet the boy was guiding him. He urged Hold On up from the creek's banks to the higher ground with muted signals, by shifting his weight ever so slightly. Hold On could see shadowy images. They were blurred, but it was more than he had seen since the fire in the canyon. He began to trot and still the boy did not try to hold his mane or fling his arms around his neck. He might as well have been carrying a feather on his back. Hold On broke into a gallop and still the boy kept a perfect balance despite his short, weak leg.

He puts no saddle on my back, no bit in my mouth, not even a rope, but with this boy I could go far. He is my eyes. Mis ojos. He neighed, then nickered. *Mis ojos!*

Tijo cocked his head and listened. It sounded as if Hold On had almost said his name. *We have named each other!* he thought happily, and stroked Hold On's shoulder. *I am not lonely! I can live without a village. And I am not a ghost, not in the blind eyes of Hold On. In his eyes I am a boy — and not just a lame boy.*

CHAPTER 7

Finished with Away

A cold wind swept down upon them and steel-gray clouds were building in the west. Estrella saw Bobtail squint and peel back his lips. Some said that the bright bay stallion had a weather eye, but it was more a weather nose. Bobtail's scent organs were large; his dark muzzle was much broader than that of most horses.

Estrella watched the stallion nervously now. He'd caught something that made him pin back his ears. She hoped with all her might that it wasn't the scent of decaying flesh — Hold On's carcass rotting somewhere.

"Bobtail," she asked, barely concealing her anxiety. "You don't smell something dead, do you?"

"No," he said, flaring his nostrils and dancing to the side. "Though I wish it were dead."

"What do you mean?"

"What I smell might be human." The stallion cast a baleful eye at Estrella. The meaning was clear. *We should have left off this useless hunt earlier.*

The word *human* sent a tremor through the herd. The horses began tossing their heads, their manes gusting up past the ears they'd pinned flat to their skulls.

"Then we have to leave!" the colt Sky said. His eyes were frantic as he thought of how his legs had been hobbled by the ropes of the Ibers. The feeling of their lariats settled like snakes around his neck.

The other colt, Verdad, jigged in place, as if struggling to keep his legs from dashing off on their own. "I was broken once by those fool Ibers. Never again. You don't know what it's like, Estrella."

"Yes, I do. They tried to break me at the City of the Gods." They had "twitched" her muzzle with a rope twisted over her upper lip, and hobbled a front foot to a hind one. The memory of the pain, the sudden loss of balance, flared throughout her entire body.

"That doesn't count!" Verdad shot back. "It's time to stop looking. Are you trying to get us all killed? You are no leader. You're just a filly."

"You think because I am a filly I cannot lead!" Estrella shook as she fought the urge to charge the colt.

A silence fell upon the herd. After a long moment, Grullo began to speak. "Estrella, you are the one who first shared your vision of the sweet grass, but now it calls to all of us. We promised that we would wait one more day for Hold On. That day ends when the sun sets this evening." Grullo's head dropped, as though it'd taken a great deal of energy to say the words.

The tide of anger welling up in Estrella's belly began to subside. Now wasn't a time for anger; it was a time for meadow wisdom. It suddenly became very clear to Estrella what she must do. Grullo was right. Their quest was about more than finding the sweet grass and filling their bellies. Bobtail had picked up the scent of humans! Humans with saddles and bits and bridles, the very things that would make a mockery of any notion of being free or wild. It was the knowledge of human cruelty that had always made Estrella carry on, carry on despite the loss of her dam, and now despite the loss of her dearest friend. They had been hobbled, tethered, beaten, thrown into shark-infested waters, tricked into entering a fiery canyon. There was no choice but to go on. It was time to go. It was time to lead.

"Now!" she said suddenly, forcing all other thoughts from her mind. The horses looked at her with confusion. "We need to go now! Right now! Move north!"

If anyone had asked how two such different creatures — a horse and a human — communicated, it would have been difficult to explain. It would have been as hard to comprehend as the wonder of a flower blooming in the snow, or a star that suddenly shoots across the sky, or those mysterious illusions that grow from the light passing through layers of quivering heat. For although Tijo used no bit, and spoke sounds Hold On had never heard, they had come to understand each other almost completely.

Tijo was as astonished as Hold On. It was nothing short of miraculous. They were communicating through a combination of touch, gesture, and soft, nearly wordless sounds. Sounds that were like music brought by the wind when it flowed through a canyon or stirred the leaves of a tree.

Tijo would often signal Hold On to stop near a certain tree or cactus, then slip off his back to strip off a leaf, scrape off a handful of bark, or collect the syrup from which he made the salves for Hold On's eyes. Soon, Hold On became adept at smelling out just the kinds of vegetation that Tijo liked for his pack, and would begin to slow down even before Tijo signaled him.

Hold On could also smell weather hours before it arrived. One afternoon he began to snort harshly. *Bad storm!* Hold On felt Tijo shift his weight as he pressed his knees against the stallion's sides and leaned back slightly. This was the signal to stop.

Hold On halted, then felt Tijo stand straight up on his back. It had surprised Hold On the first time the boy did this, as no Iber had ever stood up on his back. But this boy with one leg shorter than the other did it as if it were the most natural thing in the world. He could walk the long distance of Hold On's back from his withers to the dock of his tail, which he was doing now as he scanned the western horizon.

But Tijo saw nothing. Hold On peeled back his lips and inhaled a great mouthful of air. Tijo knew this was how the creature smelled things. He tried to do the same. Hold On shook his head and made a soft nickering sound. Tijo sensed his amusement. Hold On stopped and pawed the ground as if to say, *Trust me, it's coming.*

"Snow?" Tijo seemed to exhale the word more than actually speak it.

Hold On snorted with frustration. Weather he had always been able to abide, but this weather would wipe out other scents. It would destroy any chance of picking up the scent of his herd for days. If it was rain, it would wash the scent away completely.

Snow and something more, Tijo thought. He felt a wetness in the air, and something else. The scent of rotten eggs. The scent that Hold On had picked up much earlier.

Tijo pressed his knees to Hold On's sides and reached

forward to rub where his singed forelock fell. It was a reassuring, comforting gesture. *Don't worry. I'll find a cave. We will be safe.*

There was a grove of trees nearby, but that would be the most dangerous place to seek shelter. The rotten egg smell meant lightning. If it struck a tree, even just a branch, the tree could explode into fire, especially if it was a sap tree like the piñons. That same tree that had saved Hold On's eyes could destroy both boy and horse during a lightning storm.

They moved on toward a ridgeline of a large escarpment that faced east, away from the weather. Despite Hold On's dire predictions, the sun was still bright in the sky. Tijo spotted a long shadow up ahead that could indicate an overhang and possibly a cave.

That way. Tijo tapped his right toe gently against Hold On's shoulder and they continued. The sky was becoming angry, smoldering with thick, nearly black clouds. Tijo craned his neck and spotted the dark void in the rock wall beneath the ridgeline. He urged Hold On forward. It was a cave, a deep cave, and they entered just before the fierce gusts of wind brought the first raindrops.

Hold On pinned back his ears. His muzzle began to twitch as a terrible stench filled the air. He felt Tijo tense on his back.

Vampire bats! Hold On shuddered as a terrible image flashed through his mind.

By this time the clouds had unleashed their fury. Lightning was slashing the sky. "Some choice," Tijo muttered. "Fried by lightning or sucked bloodless by bats." He began to rub Hold On on the crest of his neck.

"Hold On, listen to me. You cannot sleep. They don't often suck humans' blood, but they love big warm-blooded animals like you. I'll stay up and try to beat them off if you sleep. You see, the cut they make is so small that you would never notice it. There is something in their bite that numbs the skin — that is what Haru told me. Numbs the skin but lets the blood flow."

Hold On pushed his ears forward. They trembled slightly. *But when will you sleep? How can I protect you?*

"They don't often attack humans," Tijo repeated, scratching Hold On between his ears.

Often could be once, and once could be bad. A shudder passed from Hold On's withers to his shoulders, as if the entire cloth of his skin flinched.

"But you can't see them, Hold On."

I'll hear them when they come near. I'll . . . I'll . . . I'll give them a licking they won't forget.

"Licking?" This was a word that Tijo had never heard the stallion use.

Hold On himself was startled. It was an Iber word. How often he had seen an Iber approach a mule with a whip coiled in his hand and a dark look as angry as the sky was outside, swearing about giving that mule a licking the creature would never forget. *Terco*, that was the Iber word for a willful and obstinate mule. He had seen mules' backs torn to bloody strips by cruel owners.

We'll both stay up together. Hold On was firm.

"If you say so," Tijo replied, and patted his shoulder, which had flinched moments before.

I say so. Hold On snorted.

They heard a stirring in the ceiling above them. Were the bats rousing? A wave of tension pulsed from Hold On's withers down his shoulders. The horse pinned back his ears, then relaxed them again and swiveled each one slowly, like figures in a lovely dance. A calm began to steal through Tijo and he reached down and rubbed Hold On's withers and whispered his name.

The stallion was an old horse and a very tired horse. He felt his eyelids grow heavy. Tijo decided it couldn't hurt to let him sleep for just a bit. He dismounted, stretched, then walked to the cave entrance, looking out at the storm-choked night. A spiderweb of lightning filigreed the sky. The full moon was rising timidly in the east. Slow in its ascent, it seemed to be dodging the fiery claws of the lightning by hiding behind the dark clouds.

Suddenly, the lightning sheeted and the sky bleached white. A strange silhouette appeared on the crest of a hillock.

"Horse?" Tijo whispered to himself. But its ears were too long, its back too short, its rump too high. What was it? Just then Tijo heard a shrill cry and a thunderous noise from inside the cave.

He ran back in, but it was too late.

CHAPTER 8

Yazz

A mule looked out into the night fractured by lightning. Was she a fool standing out here flicking her ears, tempting the fiery fates that raged overhead? The storm had taken her by surprise when she reached the summit of the hill. It had rained earlier that day, but she thought it was finished. Perhaps the storm was a blessing. It might discourage the men from pursuing her.

The lightning, particularly that last thunderbolt that whitened the night, had given her a very good sense of the shape of things. Seconds later, two spiky prongs had flashed down and ignited a stand of cottonwood trees growing beside a stream. The flames now reached up through the driving rain.

None of this frightened the mule. Not the rain, not the

flashing bolts of light, not the fire. After what had happened in the corral that day, Yazz had moved beyond shock. She was imperturbable. Was she simply too old to be shocked? There was no denying she was old — at least twenty years old — but it was not just a matter of age.

It had begun with the new owner. He had balked at the price Yazz's old owner was demanding. "She's a mule," he had argued. *"Ninguna ascendencia, no posteridad."* She had no ancestry, no future descendants. It was half-true. As a mule, she could not reproduce. She was sterile. But she did have ancestry; her sire had been a donkey and her dam a fine Iber Jennet, though it was true there would be no future generations with her blood running through their veins. But even if she could reproduce, Yazz wondered what she would be reproducing for. So some cruel owner could work a foal of hers to exhaustion in a jerkline, hauling Iber silver? There was no doubt that this new owner was one of the cruelest she'd ever had. His title was Governor but some called him El Miedo, which meant The One Who Is Feared in the language of the Ibers.

El Miedo's expedition was the largest ever launched into the New World. Its size dwarfed that of the Seeker's, who had come with fewer than a dozen ships, one hundred men, and seventeen horses. El Miedo had the king's ear and a thousand merchants' purses for this endeavor — a search for silver mines that would make them all rich beyond belief.

Earlier in the day, El Miedo had become infuriated with a mule in the jerkline and began to beat the poor thing mercilessly. Yazz had stood by helpless until the mule collapsed in a bloody heap, her back in shreds. The rain had started before her body was removed, washing the blood into red rivulets that streamed around Yazz's own hooves as the proud stallion recently captured by El Miedo walked by.

"What are you doing?" he asked. Their master called him El Noble. But to the other animals, he insisted on being called Pego.

"She is dying. To die alone is a terrible thing," Yazz replied.

"She's a mule! Mules are constructed differently. They are incapable of such feelings. They are not like *Pura Raza*, Pure Bloods."

"I am a mule. I know what a mule is capable of!"

Pego merely snorted and walked on.

"Call yourself a pure blood. I call you a pure idiot," Yazz muttered, and turned back to soothe the mule. Jenny was her name, a popular name for female mules. "You are going to a better place. You are Jenny," Yazz had softly brayed to her throughout the hours she lay dying.

The other horses and mules had wandered over to some makeshift shelters as the rain beat down harder. But Yazz would not budge from Jenny's side. Her breath by this time had become ragged. There were long spells when Yazz thought she had breathed her last breath.

During Jenny's last hour on earth, the rain had stopped, revealing a sky powdered with stars. A special constellation, *El Mulo*, the Mule, had risen that night. Perhaps that was a good sign for the dying mule, Jenny.

Yazz's own mother had told her about the star picture. "See, Yazzy," her dam had murmured. "See the design of the stars. See the long ears. See how the mule bucks. No horse can buck like a mule, Yazzy. You have bigger muscles. You have more power in your hindquarters."

"But you are so beautiful," Yazz had replied. "Your neck curves like the dipping stars."

"You are beautiful, too, Yazzy, in your own way."

"I have funny-looking hooves," Yazz said, peering down at her oddly shaped, tiny feet. Her dam's hooves were larger and had a lovely roundness that she envied.

"But you are stronger, Yazz. And those hooves make you more sure-footed. You will be able to go places I could never go. Steep-sided slopes, up and down, and never fall." Her dam paused. "Beauty can't do that for you. And you are much smarter."

But I want to be pretty, Yazz thought, looking up at the star mule. "How come it doesn't carry a pack? How come it isn't in a jerkline?"

"He doesn't wear a pack because he has laid down his burden. He is free now and can buck and romp all over *cielo de encanto*."

"But that is where dead horses go. If I am a mule and you are a horse, when I die, will we be in separate skies?"

"No! No!" Yazz's mother nickered softly, shook her head, and thought, *This is what it is like to have such a smart foal.* She was just not bright enough to answer some of Yazz's questions.

Yazz had continued to look down at her own hooves. She was such an odd combination of things — a little bit of horse, not enough. A lot of donkey, a bit too much. And where were all these brains going to get her? In a jerkline hauling Ibers' burdens — their tools, their precious metals, their food.

A light breeze blew through the corral, taking the spirit of Jenny, leaving quietly growing resolve within Yazz. She looked up at the star mule and whispered, "Why wait until I die to set aside this burden? Go now!" She felt the first hints of freedom like a telltale wind.

Her dam's words came back to her. "No horse can buck like a mule, Yazzy. You have bigger muscles, more power in your hindquarters." She looked at the corral. Why had she never even dared think of leaving until this moment? *Leave now before another helpless beast is beaten to death.* There was a place on the north side where the wood was rotting. It would be easy.

She trotted over to it. "Hey, where you going?" a donkey asked.

"Out." A mare turned around and blinked at her curiously and went back to the feeding trough. Yazz wheeled her rump around and bucked as hard as she could, kicking out at the split rails of the corral. It took only three kicks for the rails to break wide open, leaving a nice mule-size gap. Every animal in the corral was stunned. Yazz was the oldest of the mules. The steadiest. The most reliable in the jerkline. The most obedient. Why would she do such a thing? An Iber came running from the tent where El Miedo's top lieutenant slept. He had a lasso coiled in his hand and was about to unfurl it when Yazz wheeled about, charged him, and then bucked. The Iber dropped to the ground as Yazz bolted into the night.

That had been three nights ago. She could not believe how much terrain she had covered. She was amazed at how fast she could gallop without a pack of rocks, for that was what they had been carrying for the most part.

And now Yazz stood on the crest of this butte and looked at the sky crackling with lightning and thought, *This is my palace and it is lined with silver. I am free. Free!*

CHAPTER 9

One Bloody Night

Tijo raced to the back of the cave where Hold On was rearing. He had to dodge his hooves. The air was thick with gusts from the mad flapping of the bats' wings. He screamed at the bats and flailed his arms. Hold On's face was a mask of blood. Three bats hung from his chest, another two from his neck. Tijo swatted them until most flew away, although Tijo shuddered as one brushed against his skin.

A sharp whinny tore the night, anguished and accusatory, for indeed Tijo had let Hold On sleep.

Tijo approached him carefully. He knew he had to get onto Hold On's back to get them out of the cave, but Tijo was nowhere near the mounting rock.

Somehow, though, he managed to scramble onto Hold On just as the bats returned. He scraped a bat from Hold On's withers, then tapped lightly with his heels. Hold On galloped out of the cave with bats clinging to his chest and neck. It was still raining hard, but the rain had never felt so good. Tijo beat most of the bats off in less than a minute. The horrid creatures staggered into the night; their furry wings were quickly soaked, which made flying difficult for them. Tijo leaned down and scraped the last one from Hold On's flank.

No more caves! Hold On snorted.

"No more," Tijo agreed.

Hold On kept flinching his ears and shaking his head as if to vanquish the sound of the flapping wings.

Tijo removed the strip of buckskin he wore around his head and used it to mop the blood from Hold On's face. There were salves in his pack that would stop the bleeding, but to his dismay, he realized he had left the pack in the cave. He would have to return, for the pack had Haru's pipe as well as the piñon salve.

Tijo stroked Hold On with the buckskin and hummed a soft tune that Haru had sung to him. The stallion understood that Tijo had to go back into the cave, and began to tremble. Tijo pressed his cheek to Hold On's face, then snapped the band of the slingshot that hung from his waist, to indicate that the bats were no match for him.

The rain had stopped completely by the time Tijo walked back out of the cave with his pack and headed to where he had left Hold On. He inhaled sharply and stopped in his tracks. Ahead in a shaft of moonlight a figure made its way toward them. The long-eared creature he had spied on the crest was moving down the slope. It was like a horse but not quite. Tijo was frightened and came up beside Hold On. There was a sudden wind shift and the stallion caught the odor. He neighed tentatively. The new creature trotted forward, making odd noises that were not quite whinnies, but flat honks almost like those of geese. Their conversation left Tijo lost.

The longer he looked at the creature, the more peculiar it appeared. Its back had a deep sway to it. The hooves were ridiculously tiny and its ears ridiculously long. The creature was an odd assemblage of parts that did not seem to match.

Her name is Yazz. Hold On gave a nod of sorts toward the creature but seemed slightly wary. Tijo pressed his face close to Hold On.

"But what is she?"

A mule. She escaped from a cruel Iber called El Miedo with many horses and many mules. She was tired of hauling rocks in a jerkline. It's a brutal life being a mule, even with a good master.

Yazz turned to Tijo and, blinking her eyes, gave her odd whinny. "The boy speaks horse?"

"Not exactly," Hold On replied. "But not Iber." He paused and lay back his ears slightly. "Are there Iber near?"

"I can see he is not Iber. And the Iber are not near. You

need not worry." Yazz took a step closer and blinked again. Tijo blinked back. They had never quite seen each other's kind. They both had the same thought. *So close to something I know but not exactly.*

Yazz then said something that Tijo didn't understand. He was captivated by her huge shining eyes, so dark and glossy that they reflected his own face as clearly as the black water in a still pond. Hold On's eyes were mostly cloudy, filled with a perpetual mist. Sometimes, Tijo could glimpse a reflection, but nothing like the face he was now seeing.

Although Tijo was unsure what a mule was, exactly, he found the creature to be a comforting presence. He had not felt lonely since he met Hold On, but now he felt they were somehow more complete. The moon rose higher and Tijo felt as if they were wrapped in a cocoon of silver light.

The three of them walked on a few paces. The fury of the storm had subsided and an unearthly peace had descended upon them. The stars spilled with light and as they moved on with Tijo atop Hold On, they spoke occasionally but more often fell into the long elliptical silences that had no need to be filled with words. It was clear that Yazz would be joining them.

Hold On had explained to Yazz that they were heading north in hopes of reuniting with Estrella and the herd and to find the sweet grass.

They crossed a high plain, a cold relentless wind cutting across it like a blade. Hold On and Yazz huddled close together as they walked. Tijo stretched himself as flat as possible on the stallion's back to lessen the resistance against the wind. The way often became rough and uneven with rock and rubble. Yet the small-footed Yazz was as steady as any creature. It was a lonely, shelterless place, but they continued.

Over the course of the next several days, the silence was broken more frequently and Tijo began to understand the strange voice of the mule. Hold On was very curious about El Miedo and especially the vast herd that this terrible man had brought with him. He wondered if any of his friends from the old country were among them. Yet Tijo didn't understand all of it, and was surprised when Hold On suddenly stopped in his tracks, nearly sending Tijo flying over his head.

"Pego! You say this El Miedo has a stallion called *Pego?*"

"El Miedo does not call him that, but the stallion claims he was named for the star horse Pegasus."

"I know Pego. Believe me, if his master is as cruel as you say, he has found himself the perfect horse. Together, they will be deadly."

From then on, Tijo could feel Hold On's apprehension

grow. Countless times a day, Hold On would turn around and try to catch a· scent on the wind — the scent of humans, and the dark, treacherous stallion called Pego.

"Do not worry, my friend," Yazz said when Hold On stopped to sniff the air the next morning. "That is not the scent of Iber. What we must look out for is the bobcat."

"Bobcat?" Hold On's ears shoved forward as he shuddered.

"Yes," Yazz said. "Smaller than mountain lions but smarter and very sly. Like coyotes."

Tijo understood fragments of this exchange. "Bobcats!" He curled his hand into a half-open fist. His fingers clawed the air like fangs. Yes, he knew about bobcats. They were ferocious, much more intelligent than mountain lions and more savage than any coyote. In the village, they called them baby killers, for they were known to sneak into lodges and snatch babies from their cradleboards. Haru herself had lost a child to a bob-cat. It had dropped from a tree and ripped the cradleboard right off the mother's back.

"But now I have you," she had said, trying to comfort Tijo after the story made him cry.

"But maybe you could have had both of us, and I would have had a friend, a brother."

"True," Haru said in a wistful voice. At that moment, Tijo vowed that someday he would grow big enough and strong enough and clever enough to trap and kill a bobcat.

Hold On was listening carefully as Yazz described how bob-cats had attacked the Iber encampment and killed a foal.

"So we have two common enemies — the bobcats and the Ibers," Hold On said grimly.

"Though it is not our enemies that count, but our friends," Yazz said. "I think I have two friends here." She looked steadily at Hold On, then swung her head toward Tijo. Hold On sighed. His ears relaxed and he swished his tail.

"Yes, friends. You have two friends here. For this boy is like no human you have ever met."

"I believe you," Yazz said quietly.

Hold On knew a bit about mules, but he had never really understood about life on a jerkline, which sounded worse than any life he could imagine for a horse. The bridles, the whips, and the spurs he had known were nothing compared to the horrible instruments of the jerkline with its yokes across their withers. There could be anywhere from eight to twenty ani-mals in one line and they were not all mules.

"Yes, some were horses. Of course not fine stallions like you, Hold On."

"No need to flatter me."

"I'm not flattering you. They saved pure breeds like yourself for battle and parades. You were bred for speed and agility." Yazz sighed. "The peculiar creature that was created when a donkey and a Jennet were mated was bred for strength rather than speed.

For stability, steadiness of foot. That's why our hooves are shaped the way they are. And we have a certain *mild* temperament."

"But why finally did you decide to leave? What gave you the courage?" Tijo asked.

"Why do we all leave?" Yazz replied, looking at Hold On. There was a long pause.

"To be owned," Hold On said, "is unnatural."

"Yes, even now, I can still feel the yoke like a shade across my shoulders. I feel the bang of the bar against my hock and the chafe of the rings on my back. I can even feel the ghosts of my yoke mates."

"Those things will fade," Hold On said. "You must try to forget."

"Yes, I know," Yazz said. "But the real challenge is to try and discover new things to remember." There was a sparkle in the mule's eyes.

Yazz was right, Hold On thought to himself. There were so many things he wanted to remember from his travels with the first herd since coming to the New World, things he missed — not just Estrella, but the cozy natterings of Corazón and Angela, the solid common sense of Grullo, the dreamy looks that sometimes passed across the colt Sky's face with his one eye that was as blue as the sky and the other that was as dark as night. Those things he did not want to forget.

Tijo was silent for a long time as the two creatures talked. He did not want to forget everything. He did not want to forget Haru. He didn't want to forget all the stories she had told him, the songs she had sung him to sleep. Haru had taught him how to bring down swifts with a slingshot and how to slow-roast them in their feathers over a cedar fire. There were so many things she had taught him that he was not willing to let slip away.

It was now the heat of the day, and they had settled under the spreading branches of a cottonwood. When the sun slipped farther down, Tijo would go to the creek with a fishing jig he had fashioned to try for some trout. Fish did not interest Hold On or Yazz. They ate only grasses. *We are so different*, Tijo thought.

Tijo became more anxious as Hold On grew more intent on finding Estrella and the first herd. What would they think of him? After all the stories Tijo had heard of cruel masters who put bits in horses' mouths or yoked mules' shoulders and tethered them to a jerkline, he worried what these horses would do when they saw him. *I am the enemy*, he thought.

Yet each day, he understood more and more of the talk between Hold On and Yazz. They called it horse language, although Yazz had a slightly different accent or perhaps a word or two might vary.

His own language began to fade away to the point where, on occasion, he even dreamed in the horse tongue, and he could not help but wonder if he was becoming more horse than human. But what would happen if the herd abandoned him? What would he do if he was spurned and cast out? To return to the clan that had all but rejected him when he was under Haru's protection was unthinkable. However, there was nothing he could do. The choice would be theirs — the choice of the first herd.

CHAPTER 10

"What Am I Really?"

It was the first dawn after the search for Hold On ended. They had not traveled far, stopping just before first light since the ground was broken and not made for galloping. Estrella had been grazing a bit away from the herd. She did not regret her decision to end the search for Hold On, but nothing could fill a void beside her, the ghost of a companionship that once had been.

There was a piece of Estrella's mind that would always seek the sound of the stallion's hooves, the pounding of his huge heart when he galloped beside her, the keenness of the whinny with which he greeted each new day in this world of freedom.

The wind shifted slightly and began to build. Clouds were

churning in a low seeping arc. She turned around and saw that the colt Sky had moved a bit closer. Sky paid her no heed but shoved his ears forward. A confusing scene blew in on the edges of a gust.

"What is it?" Estrella asked as she caught the complicated scent. It was like a horse but not quite. Then a third scent assaulted their nostrils — sweat! Human sweat. The colt and the filly laid back their ears and stood trembling.

"It can't be!" Sky said.

"Don't panic," Estrella said. She peeled back her lips and rotated her ears in opposite circular patterns, twitching from her withers to her shoulders, as if invisible flies were biting her. The odor was coming closer. Soon she heard the hoofbeats of Grullo, Arriero, and the rest of the herd.

"What is it?" Arriero asked.

"It's boy sweat," Corazón replied. "Just one human, one boy."

"But the other scent?" Estrella asked.

"Mule," Angela said.

"Or donkey." Grullo peeled back his lips.

"No, I think mule," Angela said firmly.

Estrella had no idea what they were talking about. "Mule? Donkey?" she said, confused.

Corazón stepped forward and turned to the others. "Estrella was foaled on the ship. There were no mules on the Seeker's ship, remember."

Suddenly, an intensely familiar scent threaded through the air. "Hold On! It's Hold On!" Estrella dashed out at a mad gallop toward her old friend.

"It's Hold On," she whinnied shrilly, then stumbled in shock. A human was on his back, and the stallion's proud head seemed to droop as if sniffing the ground beneath his feet. Was it with shame? The magnificent silvery tail that had flashed behind him like a comet when he galloped was a charred stump. He was painfully thin and his broad chest appeared to have shrunk. And this human was perched on his back!

Hold On himself felt as if he had been struck by a thunderbolt. One minute the filly he had known so well was whinnying a joyous greeting and rushing toward him, and then there was a terrible skidding sound. She was stopping. She could not come near. The stallion knew what she had seen. What stopped her.

He began to buck, not hard, but the message was clear to Tijo. *Off! Off, Tijo! Off my back.*

That message was the last one Tijo could understand. Something had happened to their language. It felt as if it was dissolving. The sounds and gestures were becoming separated from the meaning.

The young filly stared in disbelief at Hold On. *Is this a dream?* Estrella thought. Could it possibly be real? She took a hesitant step forward and stretched out her neck. Then, peeling back her lips, she inhaled deeply the pungent tang of Hold On.

And the stallion, too, savored the grassy redolence of Estrella. Hold On's sense of smell was so keen now, it was as if the short but complex history of Estrella's life was revealing itself through her scent. There was the fragrance from her dam Perlina's milk. There was the salt of the sea. There was the damp thick smell of the jungle far to the south through which they had trekked, and the dust of the plains as well as the ash of the canyon fire. It was all there. But there was also the scent of fear. Hold On could hear her rapid breathing and the nervous snorts of confusion as Estrella cautiously approached him. Then, within seconds, they were nuzzling each other, wallowing in this ocean of scent.

Tijo stood apart, wobbling slightly. He felt incomplete, and for the first time in days, he was aware of his lameness. He looked longingly at those four strong legs of his friend that had carried him so far. He felt the gaze of the other horses settling upon him.

Yazz regarded the stallion and the filly and felt their joy, then turned her attention to the other horses. They were all so beautiful. Even though their coats were rough with burrs and some of their manes were singed from the canyon fires, they were sleek and magnificent. She felt ugly and ungainly. But she knew she had to step forward and do something. The tension crackled in the air like the heat lightning that sizzled low on the horizon and signaled distant thunderstorms. The two other stallions were stiff with near rage at the sight of a human. Their flashing eyes radiated danger. The two old mares were trembling with fear. The colts appeared ready to bolt.

Yazz knew that the horses were shocked to see a human, let alone one riding without bit or saddle. She felt for the boy. Tijo scuttled off a short way, his lame leg dragging like the wing of a wounded bird.

Yazz began to speak in her odd voice, which began like a whinny, then slid into a swooping hee-haw. "You are correct. No bit. No saddle. And yet the stallion is nearly blind." She turned and peered directly at Tijo with a questioning look and made a neighing sound closer in tone to that of a horse. "How do you and the stallion move along so well together with no bit, no reins?"

Tijo opened his hands, palms to the sky. "What is a bit?"

"He speaks horse?" Grullo asked. He was not sure precisely what the boy had said. But the rest of the herd were mumbling to each other in dismay and began to toss their heads nervously.

"I don't believe he can understand us," Corazón murmured.

"But I think he does, dear," Angela whispered.

"Never," Bobtail snorted.

Tijo nodded at the chestnut stallion.

The horses backed away. It was as if a freak had wandered into their midst.

Yazz took a few slow steps toward Tijo. "Would you care to show these horses how you can ride? Slip onto my back."

"Mules are a peculiar lot," Bobtail muttered.

"That we are," Yazz replied cheerfully, and then did something none of them had ever before witnessed. The mule sank onto one knee, lowering herself so the child with the crooked leg could mount her easily.

Tijo slipped onto the mule's back as the others watched in stunned silence. The boy did not make the mouth clicks with his tongue as the Ibers often did. His heels did not dig in. His arms hung loose and did not even grasp the mule's mane. But the mule moved, first in a simple trot, and then slid into a gallop. Something was transpiring between the boy and the mule, for the mule had begun to trace intricate figures, loops and curving shapes. All the while the boy sat in a perfect balance that none of them had ever seen in a rider. They even began to wonder if he was a "rider." He had in some way simply merged with the mule. Estrella saw all this. She sensed this fusion. The boy and the mule had each become more than the sum of their parts.

Hold On stood attentive but trembling. His hearing was so sensitive that he could almost see the figures that Tijo and Yazz were making. Could the herd see what he understood about this boy? Could Tijo gain their trust in this moment?

"He doesn't even have a rope on his neck," Grullo said.

"Of course not," Hold On replied curtly.

"But how does he do it?" Corazón jerked her head as if she was recalling the bridle and the bit.

"It's a mystery," Hold On replied. "Like all the best things." He held his head high and whinnied. "Come back, Tijo. Show them how you can ride an old blind and very foolish stallion."

"It's impossible," Sky snickered.

"I don't know what to make of it." Grullo shook his head rapidly, as if the answer would somehow fall out of his mane like a burr.

Yazz trotted over, and in one smooth motion, Tijo slid from the mule's back onto the stallion's. Hold On was more than ready to have him ride.

Off they streaked across the landscape. Together the boy and the horse galloped in ever more complex loops, with Hold On leaping right over stands of scrub. His timing was flawless and yet the horses saw no signals pass between the boy and the stallion. It was simply astonishing.

Astonishing and disturbing, Estrella thought. The connection between Hold On and Tijo was peculiar and vaguely threatening. There must be some trick. Something she and the rest of the herd could not see. Had the boy enchanted the stallion?

"*Brujo!*" she heard Corazón whisper to Angela. *Brujo* was an Iber word that she did not quite understand. She turned to Corazón.

"*Brujo* — what is that?"

"Witch, devil," Angela replied, and looked narrowly at the spectacle of the boy and the stallion racing across the sweep of land.

"Has he cast an enchantment on Hold On?" Estrella asked.

"It would seem that way," Corazón said with a shiver in her voice. "Magic. Dark magic."

The two words were like an ice sliver in Estrella's heart.

The first herd was astonished and nervous. Tijo and Yazz watched as they gathered in a tight huddle, a configuration they often used during winter blizzards when they turned rumps to the onslaught of the storm.

"They don't like me, I can tell," Tijo said.

"Stay calm. Let them get used to you," Yazz replied.

"What makes you think they will give me that much time?"
He did not want to say it, but he sensed that herds and clans

were probably much alike. They had their rules, their suspicions. Perhaps the whole idea was foolish from the start. How could he possibly find a home among these horses? He could not even find one among humans. Where would he go?

"It's not just you, Tijo," Yazz said. "They're skittish about me as well." Yazz could barely hear them, but she knew from the way they were staring that they had shifted their focus to her. She angled her head, stepped a bit closer, and swiveled her extremely large ears, which were twice the length of any horse's ears.

"I don't like it," Bobtail was saying. "I don't like it one bit. The boy is strange, and the mule? You know what mules are like." He turned to Corazón.

"Well, they are certainly not our . . . our . . ."

"Order," Angela said.

"They're crude," Bobtail said.

"Yazz is extremely intelligent," Hold On said.

"A mule, intelligent?" Arriero said.

"Yes, Arriero!" Hold On replied sharply, then sighed. To think that he had for so long yearned to be back with the first herd and now nothing was as he had anticipated. He turned to Estrella.

Estrella could not meet his gaze, and although she knew he could not see her clearly, she was fighting not to lay her ears back in his presence. She did not fear him. She feared these strange creatures who accompanied him.

"What do you think, Estrella?"

"I think the boy is strange, and I . . . I worry that he has . . . cast a spell on you and the mule, and that is how he can ride you."

"What?" Hold On was taken aback, though he knew what Estrella was thinking. On the evening just before the fire broke out in the canyon, a coyote had lured Estrella into the brush toward a clump of a plant — flora *loca*, it was called. She had become delusional and in her fevered dreams had thought the coyote was her dam, Perlina.

Estrella began to tremble and scratch the ground nervously with one hoof. She did not like to be reminded of that evening. She had been a fool. Now she did not know how to respond to Hold On. She could not bear the thought of Hold On thinking poorly of her. And if not for this boy, they might never have found Hold On again.

"Listen to me, all of you," Grullo said. "We have to remember that the boy has helped Hold On. He has become Hold On's eyes. Who knows what might have happened if they had not found each other?" He tossed his head with a snort.

"So before we say no to the boy and no to the mule, we should let them travel with us," Grullo said. "Give them a chance."

"One human can draw more humans," Bobtail said.

"We have to try," Grullo said emphatically.

They turned their heads to Estrella, waiting to see what she thought. Once again, she found herself in an impossible position. The boy made her uneasy — his smell, his movements — everything recalled the terrible men who'd left her dam to die in the sea. But she couldn't cast him out without betraying Hold On, the best friend she had in the world. "He can stay with us, for now. Until we decide what's best."

Despite Grullo's plea, the horses of the first herd did not take readily to the newcomers. Later that afternoon when the sun was still high, the horses settled down for a brief rest under the spreading branches of three cottonwood trees. The manner in which they had arranged themselves seemed purposely to exclude the mule and Tijo.

"Come on over here, dear," Angela said to Hold On. "It will be cooler in the shade. These late autumn afternoons can turn hot."

"No, thank you," Hold On said. "I shall stay here."

Tijo reached up and stroked his neck. *You can go.*

He neighed softly in reply. *I prefer your company.*

These four simple little words, *I prefer your company*, glowed in Tijo's mind like the brightest constellations in the sky. Tijo had said good-bye once to the person most dear to him — Haru. Saying good-bye to Hold On was unimaginable.

CHAPTER 11

"He Shall Call You Pegasus"

El Miedo was riding on his fine horse El Noble as he made his way north. It was bobcat territory, and the horses and pack animals were skittish, but not this magnificent stallion. Nothing seemed to frighten him. He had also picked up the scent of the bobcat, but bobcats did not frighten him. He had fought them off before with the help of Coyote when he traveled with Azul, the two mares, and the filly Lourdes.

In fact, the bobcats knew he was working with Coyote. And for all their cunning, and their fleetness and their strength, they feared Coyote.

Things often worked out for the best, Pego thought as he made his way through this rolling countryside braided by two rivers. It was as if the very landscape acknowledged his and El

Miedo's power, for the thin silvery grass shivered in their wake as they passed through. With El Miedo astride, they led five hundred men, eighty-three carts, twenty-four mules, and nearly six hundred horses. The parts fused into one massive creature that seemed neither man nor beast but some other force of nature, as if a torrential sea were plowing through the landscape.

Coyote had brought him to El Miedo, and El Miedo had immediately recognized Pego's quality, his nobility.

Pego only wished those pathetic horses of the first herd could see him. They had rejected him as their leader to follow the young filly Estrella. She knew nothing and yet they believed in her. Her bloodline, he could tell, was not nearly as ancient nor as pure and unsullied as his own. Her mother had been a silvery gray, and like so many pale horses, she was suspected of having what some called the Old Eye or the Eye of Time. All rubbish, of course. But they believed it.

All the horses who had ever turned from him should see him at this moment — leading more than six hundred horses, five hundred men, and fourscore wagons. He was El Noble, the horse with the greatest conquistador who ever rode now on his back, amid the jangle of the steel sword of Toledo and the creak of the wagons. They were a force that would dominate this new world.

Of course, the chances of the first herd's surviving the fire in the canyon were remote. Yet it would've almost been worth having them alive to see him now. That filly Estrella was too proud. El Miedo would have left her back in bloody ribbons, as he had the mule Jenny's. And though Bobtail was said to have been a favorite of the Seeker, he was no match for Pego. He would have been given, perhaps, to a second lieutenant.

Pego sensed that greater rewards were to come his way. El Miedo had been granted a governorship. The Seeker had not. This meant that this new world was theirs! They had found much silver already, but what they needed now to build his palace were slaves, and El Miedo had plans for that. He had sent out scouts. There were two Chitzen villages on the move, and he knew El Miedo planned to capture them when the time was right. But they also needed more horses. A dozen or more had escaped along with ten mules on the night when Yazz had kicked out the rotten rails of the corral.

Last night Coyote had come again. He slipped into the encampment and found Pego near the watering trough, the special one reserved for El Miedo's favorites. There were no others of those favorites nearby.

"Greetings," Pego neighed.

"You seem well settled," Coyote answered, and looked about casually. "This herd has dwindled. Not quite six hundred now. You are not tempted to flee as the others did the night the mule kicked down the rails of the corral?"

"No. Why should I go? I lead the greatest force in the New World. My master loves me."

"Clever," Coyote replied. "He loves you because you are like him — One to Be Feared."

Pego's withers bristled with excitement. This reaction was not lost on Coyote. "The time has come," Coyote said.

"The time for what?"

"The time for vengeance and . . . and" — Coyote's voice had dropped to a hoarse whisper — "ascendance." Coyote fancied himself a bit of a poet and often fell into rhyme. "Vengeance and ascendance," he repeated, and looked up where, if storm clouds had not roiled the sky, the star horse would be galloping through the darkness. "You are a god, are you not?" Pego felt a deep thrill and could not restrain himself from a slight nod. "Now is the time. Your time."

"How do you mean?"

"Oh, my. For a god, you have short ears sometimes. Can you not hear me? Your enemies live."

"Estrella, first herd. They survived?" Pego laid flat his ears and peeled back his lips as if searching for the filly's scent.

"Yes." There was a tone of exasperation in Coyote's reply. "Through no fault of mine. There is some solace, however. The old stallion Hold On is blind." He paused and then added in a voice dripping with sarcasm, "Shall we mourn his loss? Cry bitter tears? Oh, I forgot — horses are incapable of crying." There was a reek of nastiness that came off Coyote that would have alarmed any normal animal, but Pego was not one of those.

"Really! But what of Estrella?"

"Not a mark on her." Coyote paused. "But don't despair. Is it not clear to you? Your master, El Miedo, needs horses desperately since the mule escaped and what, fifteen, twenty horses fled? Just think of how he will love you if we lead them to the first herd. And you . . . you, my friend, will ascend. You shall become lord of the largest herd on the continent. El Miedo will have the priest bless you. He calls you El Noble now. But I promise you, when he realizes what you have done, he will — with of course a bit of help from me — look toward the heavens and see who you really are. And he shall call you Pegasus!"

Coyote did not mention the boy Tijo or that it was his own vengeance as much as Pego's that drove him. He did not say that he had been cheated of his due by Haru. That she had swiped that infant from his jaws when he had come out from his lair, hearing the boy infant's mewlings. But Coyote sought more than vengeance. He wanted power. He knew his world was changing with the arrival of these new animals called horses, with these men astride them from a distant land.

Then Coyote danced off into the night that swirled with rain and fog.

I am coyote,
I am coyote,
First Angry they call me.
I am the dream maker
and the dream taker.
You might blink
But never think
While I work my magic
To craft the tragic,
If not for me,
There would be no you.
I know your secrets,
I have no regrets,
I prey on dreams
That through you stream,
Leaving bodies
For carrion eaters.
I am the dream feeder,
I am coyote.

CHAPTER 12

Time Weavers

It was one thing being left out of a patch of shade in the hottest hours of the day. But there were now no "hottest hours." The midday sun had grown weak. There was a bite in the air. Winter in the old country was harsh even when they were brought into the stables of the Iber and were given grain every day. But the winters were much harsher here in this new world. The horses had endured one winter already in their first year. They needed one another in order to survive.

Hold On, Yazz, and Tijo had been traveling with the herd for several days now. The day before, they had stopped and gathered around a small watering hole. Arriero had twisted his head around to glance at Tijo briefly and then begun drinking. The message was clear. *Find your own watering hole.* Tijo turned away. Estrella had watched Tijo limp slowly downstream. *I don't know*, she thought, *about witches and water. But I do know about loneliness.*

The one time Tijo never felt alone was when he was riding Hold On or Yazz. It was, of course, the source of the herd's suspicions, yet they could not tear their eyes away.

"How does he command you?" Sky asked when Hold On and the boy returned with some of the plants they needed for salves.

"Tijo does not command," Hold On replied.

"I cannot believe it," Estrella said.

"You don't believe what you cannot see, eh?" Hold On said in a low, insistent voice. He had never addressed her in quite this manner. She cringed. "Watch this, Estrella."

Hold On and Tijo set off again. A thrill pulsed through Tijo. Now was the time to show this herd what they could really do. *They think* you *give me the commands!* Hold On flexed the muscles in his shoulders and shifted the cadence of his steps ever so slightly as Tijo adjusted his weight. They were approaching a narrow brook that was rushing with water. The herd watched tensely.

"You see Hold On hears the water," Yazz said.

"But how does he know how wide the creek is? There is a big rock in the middle!" Estrella gasped.

Yazz said nothing. *Let them worry.*

"What is the boy doing?" Estrella was alarmed, for now Tijo was standing up on Hold On's back. They had never seen anything like it. Hold On arched his long neck. His shoulders began to lift as he gathered all his strength. His forelegs curled tighter and the back ones flexed. Suddenly, he was airborne, as if all the stallion's energy had been uncoiled. The whole time, the boy's feet never left Hold On's back. They were both flying. None of the horses had ever seen such a leap. Not even the older ones like Grullo and Bobtail and Arriero, who were veterans of many battles.

The horses regarded the boy with a wonder untainted by suspicion. He was a different kind of human from any they had ever known. Hold On was not actually being ridden by Tijo, nor was the boy being carried, exactly, across the landscape by Hold On. They had fused into one entirely new creature. It was impossible to tell where horse left off and boy began. It was not witchcraft, but it was miraculous.

Yet despite their amazement, they were still apprehensive around Tijo. Was he human? Or part horse? Uncertainty, ambiguity confounded the herd, leaving Tijo to wonder if he was destined to be *omo* forever.

The scent of the bobcat was growing stronger. Tijo had begun to fashion blade points for his arrows and spear. He needed meat, but could these blades serve the horses, who only grazed on grasses?

It was chilly and Tijo shivered alone. Hold On and Yazz had gone in search of water, and the other horses were standing in pairs for warmth. Tijo yawned. Despite the cold, his eyelids were growing heavy. The air shuddered with the hoot of an owl.

He wondered about hunting from the back of Hold On. Would any of the other horses let him ride? It seemed unlikely. He could always build a snare, although once by mistake he had caught a ghost owl or *omo* owl. They were called ghost owls because of their white faces and were considered bad luck. The chieftain ordered him to kill it, but instead he had set it free. Luckily, the snare had not broken its wing.

Tijo heard the hoot of the owl again. He felt his body become uncommonly still, and he was overwhelmed by a strange sensation, as if his own spirit was slipping from him.

They will call that ga *in times to come.*

Tijo looked around. Someone, something had spoken. He saw his own sleeping form beneath him. *Do I wake or sleep?*

You are awake. The voice came from the branch.

Then he saw the pale, heart-shaped face of an *omo* owl. A *ghost owl.*

I am not a ghost, the owl replied. *Nor are you. We are anything but ghosts.*

What are we, then?

We are long spirits. Time weavers. We weave between the oceans of time like the shuttle of Haru's loom. We see the cloth of the future and that of the ancient past. The owl paused. *Like him.* He spun his head and appeared to flip it upside down. It almost made Tijo dizzy, but he saw what the owl was indicating. There was a tiny horse flickering in the night. *First Horse, the dawn horse. He is the one who leads the herd,* the owl said.

But who is ga?

Ga is not a who, but it is part of Hoole. Yet Hoole has not yet happened. Hoole has not yet hatched.

What is to come in the future? Tijo asked.

Oh, we are in the before of the long after. And the tiny horse, he was before the before in the first dawn of the horses.

And you see this?

I see it all and so will you, horse boy.

Those words — *horse boy* — rang like chimes in his mind and stirred Tijo's heart. *Horse boy. I am Horse Boy and not Lame Boy!*

A cold wind snapped the air. Arriero and Verdad had been traveling in an amiable silence as they scouted for a water source.

"I hope we find a stream soon," Arriero said.

"I hope we don't find a cat. Winter's coming and the meat eaters need to fatten up," Verdad replied.

Suddenly, a frantic screech ripped through the stillness. Sky, who had been trotting ahead, came charging down a slope and rushed up to them.

His one blue eye refracted a light of pure terror. "Bobcat!" he said with a shrill whinny. "Run!"

Minutes later they arrived at the encampment where the rest of the herd was resting. Panting, Sky reported what he had seen.

"We should leave immediately," Estrella said. "We'll go back to that last spring where we drank." She blinked as the herd suddenly broke into a wild gallop. She took off after them. She was the fastest runner and was soon catching up with them and then cut out to circle in front. But there was no joy to this gallop. Running felt all wrong. They had finally started moving north toward the sweet grass. They could not retreat from every threat or they'd never make it.

Skidding to a halt and rearing, she bellowed:

"No!"

The horses bumped up against one another. Hold On, with Tijo riding, and Yazz were toward the back of the herd.

"We must hunt him down," Estrella continued. "Or he will hunt *us*."

Arriero seemed taken aback by this swift decision, by the filly's boldness in the face of danger. "Yes," he said quickly. "I was thinking the same thing myself. I was about to suggest it before the rest of you broke away."

Estrella let it go. She was used to this stallion's ways. She was not going to take time to dispute him. She turned instead to Tijo.

"I have seen you working on a blade."

"Yes, I have a spear with a very sharp blade. It'll be good for bringing down a bobcat."

"You have nothing!" Bobtail said. "You will be a hindrance. It is time for the human to be left behind." He paused. "It is for your own good."

"We need the boy," Hold On said. But his words were drowned out by the squabbling horses.

Tijo felt his heart contract. Estrella smelled this fear, not the fear of a bobcat but the fear of an orphan.

"Let him stay!" Estrella whinnied loudly.

"No!" roared the three stallions, Bobtail, Grullo, and Arrierio.

I am their leader, Estrella thought. *And this is not the time to wait, to pause, but the time to go first. Go First* — the words were radiant in the filly's mind.

"He shall stay and he shall ride me!" Estrella said. A hush fell on the herd. "We will hunt the beast together."

Hold On was as stunned as the rest of the horses, but he knew that Estrella's move was brilliant. She was a true leader. The leader of this herd. Tijo slid down from Hold On and jumped lightly onto her back.

CHAPTER 13

Festering Dreams

Six days' journey away, El Miedo had finally fallen into a restless sleep. He dreamed of horses — horses he had lost, horses he must find. The land was vast and to conquer it, he needed horses. It was not just the land itself he dreamed of conquering, but the people — the Chitzen to the south and those to the north. His scouts had reported bands of people on the move. He knew they had never seen horses, and when they did, they would think he was a god.

"I need horses," he muttered in his sleep. "Thank the Virgin I did not lose the Noble One." Something stirred in his tent. El Miedo blinked. A figure loomed before him, misty except for a smear of burnished gold, and it seemed to be bowing to him.

"Indeed, Your Majesty. Thank the Virgin the noble horse is so loyal and did not flee the night the mule kicked down the fencing."

El Miedo opened his eyes wide. Was this a person or a creature? It wore what seemed to be a crown, but it had the tilted green eyes of an animal — a *perro zorro*, the dog fox! It now reared. "What do you want?" El Miedo asked in a trembling voice.

"The question is, what do you need?"

"Horses. I need horses." Was this figure was a god or a demon? Did it matter? This was an opportunity not to be wasted. Of that he was sure.

"Oh, that we know, and of course you have the best of all the horses. I brought him to you."

"Yes. Yes, of course."

"But don't you see you must think larger. What do you want? A kingdom? A crown? An empire?"

"Who are you?" El Miedo's eyes narrowed. It was as if he knew this creature — a creature torn from the fabric of his dreams? Those dreams when he had first glimpsed El Noble?

"Some call me First Angry."

"What should I do? I need horses to wrest a kingdom from the New World."

A huge gust blew up, suddenly ripping a gash in the tent just above where El Miedo slept.

Look up to the sky,
Don't ask me why.
Like the sailors at sea,
Find your way by the stars,
Don't look to the earth.
'Taint no use. 'Taint no use.
Don't stop and wonder why,
Don't stop and even think,
Don't stop to ask the way.
Let the horse stars be your guide
And then you shall abide,
There'll be new horses waiting.
Just you see. Just you see.
Find your way by the stars
In the oceans of the sky,
For the stars never lie.
You'll find your way,
Find your way.

Despite the cold, El Miedo was in a feverish sweat. He sank back on his rough pillow. Had he drunk too much of the fire-water? Was this an illusion? But the dream creature had visited him before, and the stallion had followed shortly thereafter. Was it the same creature — the *perro zorro* — or was it a true devil? The priest slept in the tent next to his. Had the priest seen it? Surely if the priest had seen it, he would be roused.

He turned his head toward the tent with the cross on top. He could hear the sonorous snores issuing forth. Sound asleep! He felt a tide of relief. But at the same time, there was an overwhelming stench. Was it the sulfurous stench of the hell-fires? No, it was merely his own sweat! *But I am not sick.* Indeed he had never felt more powerful. And now the smear of burnished gold that had awakened him suddenly seemed to take the form of a golden crown. Not a coronet worn by the lower ranks but an emperor's crown, and on top was a figure — the eagle of Castile studded with two tilting emeralds for eyes. His heart did stir as he gazed upon those emerald eyes, and the sweat poured from his brow, drenching his beard. He ran his fingertips across his brow, slick now, but the sweat was cool. Cool, he thought, like water from the baptismal font. *I am blessed, blessed by this visitor.*

CHAPTER 14

The Hunt

Tijo immediately noticed the difference between riding Estrella and Hold On. There was a fluidity to her motion that must have stemmed from the fact that her vision was intact. She moved with more assurance, confidence. The bobcat was swift and had darted up a steep slope, but they were gaining on him. Tijo felt the power of the filly's legs, the depth of her broad chest, and the immensity of that young pounding heart. He was vaguely aware of his own breath beginning to mesh with hers.

It was not as if he was guiding her. Their minds, their muscles, seemed to conspire to find the best track, the perfect speed for this hunt. There was a profound harmony building between them.

The way was rough and the land pitched down into one of the broad basins. The bobcat streaked ahead across the flat of the basin. The spots on his pelt became a smear. He was fast, but Estrella's strides were longer. Tijo hoped the land would remain treeless. If there was a tree, the bobcat could climb it in a matter of seconds, and this would definitely give him the advantage. He needed to take this animal down in open space.

The bobcat was climbing the slope on the opposite side of the basin. Seconds later it reached the summit and turned, as if daring Tijo to hurl his spear. The bobcat had the advantage. Throwing a spear uphill was harder. Perhaps the bow would be better. But before Tijo could think, the bobcat had disappeared over the edge. They could hear the sliding cascade of small rocks on the other side. Estrella didn't hesitate and took the distance to the summit in a single leap. The bobcat looked back in alarm at their sudden appearance. *Good!* Tijo and Estrella both thought.

They finally hit the flat terrain and could give chase in earnest. They were gaining on the cat. Again they were almost within range for the spear. The cat's odor came off in thick waves. Tijo crouched on Estrella's back, a stable position for launching the spear. But then the bobcat wheeled about. If there had been any fear in his eyes, it had vanished. The acrid smell, too, had vanished. The bobcat was attacking them, fangs bared. It was right under Estrella's chest. It leapt and tore at Estrella's shoulder. Blood slashed the air. Tijo dropped the spear and took his flint dagger from his belt. He was face-to-face with the large yellow eyes streaked with black. A fang slashed at his face. But Tijo felt nothing. He thrust out his knife as hard as he could. There was a crack and then an enormous spurt of blood as the cat collapsed under them.

It was over so quickly that both Tijo and Estrella were left in a daze. When he looked down and saw that the cat was truly dead, he unleashed a long quavering cry: "Haaaaaruuuuuu!"

Estrella kept up her running walk with blood still dripping from her shoulder as Tijo stared at the bloody knife he had just plunged into the bobcat's heart. He felt blood from his own face dripping onto its handle. Estrella finally slowed and then stopped.

"A thick pelt on that one. You'll be warm," the horse said as Tijo slipped from her back.

"How's your shoulder?"

"Just a scrape. How's your face?"

Tijo broke into a smile. "Just a scrape."

The rest of the horses had found some decent grass, but none were in the mood for grazing. They were too nervous. Tijo and Estrella had set off so quickly that, had the herd been tempted to follow, it was doubtful they would have kept up. And Hold On had cautioned them against going. "This is for the boy and the filly." So they stood alert for any sign of their return. It was Hold On who first heard Estrella's light, swift steps, then out of a swirl of dust, the two emerged.

"I see them! I see them!" Verdad whinnied.

"I smell blood," Hold On said with a nervous snort.

"The blood of the bobcat!" Grullo said. "They got the cat."

"And the blood of the boy and the filly!"

Tijo slipped off and ran to Hold On, pressing his bloody face to the horse's.

"No! No. I am fine. We are both fine. We got the bobcat. Don't worry. I know how to mend this," Tijo said, pointing to his cheek and then to Estrella's shoulder. "I just need Haru's medicine kit."

Luckily, there were several lengths of gut string he could use for stitching their wounds. The horses watched in amazement as Tijo washed his and Estrella's torn flesh, then used a good dose of the toothache plant powder that Haru had ground to numb torn skin. "It will sting a bit at first, Estrella," he said as he smeared it on the horse's shoulder. "But soon you won't feel anything." As he waited for the numbness to set in, he threaded a thin bone needle with the deer gut. The horses gathered around closer and watched in wonder as Tijo poked the needle into the horse's skin.

"I can't believe it!" Verdad gasped. "She isn't even flinching."

"I don't feel a thing," Estrella replied.

"I saw a blacksmith do this once," Grullo said. "A mare had cut herself on a nail in her stall, and the blacksmith sewed her up just as Tijo is doing."

The procedure was soon completed.

"Now it's my turn," Tijo said. "But I am not sure how I'll know where to stitch since I cannot see my own face."

"We could try and tell you, dear. Sort of guide you," Angela said, stepping close to him.

"Maybe," Tijo replied uncertainly. However, the mare was quite close and he saw reflected in her eyes the branches of the piñon tree behind him. "Wait! I have an idea." What had been the first thing that had astounded him when he met Yazz and then the other horses? It was their brilliant eyes in comparison to Hold On's clouded ones. He had seen his own reflection in Yazz's shining eyes that storm-torn night. And Estrella had the largest, darkest eyes of any of them. He turned to her now. The reflection of the face that looked back at him was older than he remembered.

"Estrella, come. Come close and be my mirror."

The horses watched in awe as Tijo began the procedure he had just completed on Estrella on his own face. "Don't blink," he said playfully.

"I wouldn't dare," she replied. She watched as the needle

poked in and out. The stitches were tiny, much tinier than the ones he had made for her.

Tijo felt as if he were slowly falling into the immense dark pools of the filly's eye. As during the hunt, he could hear her heartbeats and she, he knew, could hear his. Two such different hearts in size and yet hearts that seemed to whisper the secrets of their souls. Tijo could see himself more clearly than ever before. And at the same time he could see Estrella more clearly. It felt like a merging of two spirits and he thought of the *omo* owl. Was Estrella a long spirit, too? As the question formed in his mind, he caught a glimpse of the tiny horse he had seen flickering in the night when he had first met the *omo* owl. First Horse, the *omo* owl had called him, or sometimes the dawn horse. Tijo's hands worked skillfully. He felt nothing when he poked the needle in and out of his flesh. Was he stitching himself, binding himself to a deeper past? His skin was numb but he felt so alive. Yet he knew in the silence that enveloped them all that he was at last part of the herd — the first herd of the New World.

CHAPTER 15

A Weather Shelter

Tijo skinned the bobcat using his knife to separate the hide from the flesh. He was as delicate in his motions with the knife as he had been with the needle. The herd looked on in wonder as Tijo quietly went about his task. With each cut, the shadow of the bobcat that had hung over the herd receded. At first, there was just a sense of relief, but the relief soon gave way to a quiet elation and then an explosion of sheer happiness. Finally, Sky burst out with the question they were all wanting to ask.

"Will you ride me, Tijo?" Sky said, trotting in place as though he could barely contain his excitement. Tijo smiled to himself. It was the first time any member of the herd except Hold On and Estrella had ever called him by his name.

"No, me?" Verdad pushed ahead of the blue-eyed colt.

All the horses were clamoring now to be ridden by Tijo, and Tijo was as anxious to try riding them as they were to have him on their backs. He would show them when he mounted how the difference between human and horse dissolved. They would fuse into one being as he did with Hold On and with Yazz and with Estrella.

He rode Grullo first, and then Bobtail, followed by Sky and Verdad. Riding them was very different from riding Estrella. The others had been "broken" — a terrible word, Tijo thought. It was as if the ghosts of saddles and bits and bridles still haunted them. Once Tijo was on their backs, they moved differently.

Their hooves became tangled in the old gaits that Hold On had tried so hard to forget. But Sky, Estrella, and Verdad had never been broken, had never carried saddles or worn bits in their mouths. Nor had their heads been encased in bridles. When they galloped with him, it was different. He followed their lead, their instincts, and was barely aware of having to signal them at all.

A few days later, the horses were watching Estrella gallop ahead with Tijo perched on her back. He was standing upright. Corazón gasped. "Look how fast and smooth they go. They remind me of a shooting star, with Estrella's pale coat and her black mane flaring out . . ."

"Like a comet?" Hold On asked. The other horses turned to look at him.

"Hold On, can you see that?" Angela asked.

"I can see a bit more each day. I cannot see them clearly, but I can feel their wind and I can hear the hoofbeats."

"Look!" Grullo said in a startled voice. "What is the boy doing now?"

Tijo had lowered himself to sit astride Estrella and was nocking an arrow in the new bow he had made. He had spotted a red-legged grouse poking its head from its ground nest. It had come out and was running in an attempt to launch itself into flight. Grouse were clumsy runners and poor fliers. But even as clumsy as they were, they had been hard for Tijo to bring down when he had to run after them on foot. He had usually built snares. But now he did not have to run. He signaled Estrella his intentions. She accelerated, and he flattened himself on her back and took the arrow from the bow. He would use it as a spear.

The grouse was no match for Estrella. The moment the bird started to take flight, they were even with him. Tijo leaned down and with one quick jab skewered the bird. Drops of blood spun off into the clear morning air.

"You got it!" Estrella whinnied triumphantly.

· "*We* got it!" Tijo said. Tonight he would have meat, and he would save the feathers and make something lovely for Estrella. Perhaps he could braid them through her mane.

When they returned to the herd, the horses were as jubilant as Tijo and Estrella. They all wanted to carry him on a hunt now.

"Why didn't you use the bow?" Grullo asked. "You had been practicing with it for so long."

Tijo laughed. "I blame it on Estrella. She went too fast! Bows are good for long distances. Before I knew it, Estrella and I were practically on top of that bird. I realized that we would have more control if we used the arrow as a spear."

"We?" Estrella asked. "It was all you, Tijo."

"No, it's *we*. I could never have done this if not for you. If I were on the ground, I could not have run fast enough to even get a shot with my bow. Without your legs, I am just a lame boy." He looked around at the other horses. "Without any of you, I am less than whole."

Hold On stepped forward. "And we have become more, too, because of you."

"The feathers are beautiful, aren't they?" Tijo plucked one with a barred pattern of brown and black and white from the grouse's tail and took it to Estrella. "Let me braid it into your mane. It will look so pretty."

The horses gathered closer and watched Tijo's nimble fingers plait it into Estrella's black mane.

"But now you need one, too," Estrella said.

"I suppose I do." And he took another feather and twisted it into his own black hair. The horses nickered their approval.

They made camp near a stream. Streams had become more plentiful as they traveled into the high country. The weather turned and ice was beginning to form in patches on the slower-running creeks. Tijo built a small fire and roasted the bird. Between the fire and the bird's succulent meat, he was getting warm.

Hold On suddenly lifted his head toward the north and peeled back his lips, then snorted.

"What is it?" Estrella asked.

"I smell snow," Hold On said. "It's coming our way." The herd turned toward the north. Heavy blue-gray clouds had begun to roll in. There was a pale halo around the sun, and soon tiny ice crystals were swirling through the air. Tijo felt their sting on his face. The crystals began to grow until they were fat flakes. Estrella glanced at Tijo nervously. Her own coat had already grown thick for winter, but the boy seemed bare, almost naked compared to the horses. He was shivering. She could tell although he tried to hide it by wrapping his arms tightly across his chest.

All the horses looked at Tijo as the snowfall became heavier. Each had heard tales about newborn foals who'd become lost in a blizzard and froze to death. Hold On himself had lost a foal in just this manner when the colt became separated from him and the dam. Estrella knew he must be thinking of that colt now as he walked toward Tijo.

"Tonight I shall sleep lying down," he announced. "And Tijo will sleep just beside me. He will share my warmth." The horses neighed approvingly. Most often the horses slept standing up by locking their forelimb joints, the weight-bearing bones.

The horses began to move around. They would settle for a moment and then rearrange themselves. Tijo looked on somewhat confounded. It was not like the other night in the sleeping circle, where they had all settled quite quickly. Hold On would lie down, then rise up again. They were all whinnying and neighing quietly and sometimes giving the horse nearest a gentle nudge with their muzzles.

"Let's get down to business. Estrella, you go there and Bobtail here," Yazz ordered.

"What are you doing?" Tijo finally asked.

"Making weather shelter," Yazz answered. "In cold weather, we come together in standing sleep and press against one another."

"But the problem is," Bobtail said, "how do we make one for a boy? We don't want to crush the poor lad."

"We don't do it standing," Yazz said. "Well, one of us

will have to stand and keep alert. But the rest lie down. I'll show you."

Yazz began to walk in a tight circle around the campfire. She paused, struck the ground with her tiny hoof, and scraped a mark. "Here, Tijo. This is where you sleep." She moved back a bit. "And here, Hold On, lie down right here. Now over here, Grullo." Grullo moved to the spot Yazz had designated. "Verdad, you slip in there between Grullo and Arricro. Good!" Yazz said, surveying the weather shelter. "If any one of you begins to roll over in your sleep, I shall alert Tijo." She looked up at the snow, which was falling more heavily. "We don't need to worry about snow accumulating and Tijo being smothered. Your breathing will melt the snow in this circle and protect him."

It did not take long for all the horses to fall asleep. Tijo heard the rhythmic bellowing of their breaths as their huge chests rose and fell. What power surrounded him. Power and grace. He felt as if he were sheltered in the very heart of all these horses — one immense, beating heart. He looked up. Stray images passed through Tijo's mind. The snowflakes were large and fluffy and seemed to fall through the darkness like the blossoms from some night-blooming winter flower. A dusty moon rolled out from behind a cloud. For a second or two he thought he saw the shadow of an owl's wings printed against the moon's face. An *omo* owl, perhaps? The wings dissolved into the night. The snow lessened, darkness surged. The moon was naked and silvery. The patches of shadows on its surface appeared to shift slightly, rearranging the moon's face into a different one. A pair of familiar eyes loomed out. "Haru?" he whispered into the darkness. But there was only silence. Silence and the comforting snores of the herd.

CHAPTER 16

Bella!

By morning, the landscape had been transformed. Hillocks had disappeared under the thick mantle of snow. The cottonwoods stooped, their snow-laden branches dragging on the ground as if old and lame.

Arriero and Sky set out ahead of the rest of the herd to scout once again for a good water source, one that was not frozen, for the night had been a bitter one. Plumes of snow exploded in their wake.

They had not gone far when Arriero stopped short.

"What is it?" Sky's withers flinched and a small cascade of snow fell from them. "Another bobcat?" Seconds later he picked up the scent as well. It was slightly familiar.

"Horse!" Arriero said.

"Is it . . . is it . . . Pego?" Sky stammered.

"Not exactly," Arriero said. Ahead was a small bluff. From behind a boulder the gaunt figure of a mare shambled from the shadows of large rocks.

"Bella?" they both said at once. Bella was the mare of Pego, the stallion who had betrayed the first herd.

Sky started to trot toward her.

"Wait! Wait, Sky, it could be a trick."

The colt immediately stopped. "She looks sick, Arriero."

The mare caught sight of them and gave a frail whinny. She began to walk toward them and then stumbled.

"She's alone," Arriero said. Her own scent was strong, and overpowered any lingering odor of the treacherous Pego. Still, they were wary, and moved slowly as the mare approached.

"Forgive me? Can you forgive me?" Her knees began to buckle and she collapsed on the ground.

"What happened to your foal?" Arriero asked.

"Dead. Born dead," she replied weakly.

"And Pego?" Sky asked.

"He left." Her voice was flat and her eyes dull.

"How could he leave?" Sky asked, his voice full of mingled horror and disbelief.

"I was useless if I couldn't give him offspring. He's proud. Proud of his bloodline, you know that. But can you forgive me?"

"For what?" Sky asked. The colt was confused.

"We led you into that canyon . . . the fire . . . and . . . all."
Her voice was growing weaker.

"It was Pego, not you," Arriero said staunchly.

"I don't know. I don't care. I want to die and join my foal.
My colt. It was a colt. The vultures came immediately. I fought
them off as best I could. But I was too weak. They stripped that
bright little fellow to the bone. He had a tawny coat like mine.
Only bones left. Only the bones." Her voice dwindled like a
guttering flame.

"You don't want to die!" Arriero spoke fiercely.

"I am nothing. I am empty."

Arriero and Sky glanced at each other frantically. "You are
something. You can be part of our herd. First herd."

"We won't leave you here," Sky said. "We won't leave you
for the vultures."

Arriero decided to stay with Bella while Sky raced back to
the herd's meeting place. Tijo had medicines. Medicines had
helped Hold On. *They could help Bella*, thought Sky, shuddering
as he tried to wrap his mind around Pego's cruelty. The stallion's
deceit knew no bounds, and his treachery was never-ending.

"What in the world?" Corazón looked up to see Sky tearing
through the snow. He skidded to a stop. His ears were laid flat
and he panted several times, catching his breath.

"You won't believe it!" Sky gasped.

"What?" Grullo asked tensely.

"Bella!"

"Bella." Angela gave a shrill whinny. "Pego's mare!"

"Pego's not with her," Sky said, still gasping for breath. The horses were pressing around him now. They were nervous, swiveling their ears, peeling back their lips to pick up a scent.

"Where's Arriero?" Hold On asked in an anxious voice.

"Arriero stayed with Bella . . ." The colt's voice seemed to break. "She's very sick . . . she might be dying."

"Her foal. She was expecting a foal," Corazón said slowly as the memory came back to her.

"The foal was stillborn. That's why Pego left her. He said she couldn't give him a good foal."

"And he abandoned her just like that!" Angela whinnied with disgust.

"Yes," Sky said grimly. "He left her weak and near death with the dead foal beside her." The horses stirred and snorted lowly as if trying to explain such behavior to themselves.

Sky looked at Tijo. "Tijo, you must come with your medicine kit. Maybe you can help. Arriero is waiting for you. He did not want Bella to die alone."

No, thought Tijo. *No one should die alone.* That's why he'd followed Haru out from the camps.

"Can I ride you, Estrella?" he asked.

"And I shall go along," Hold On offered.

Tijo leapt onto Estrella's back. He must be getting taller, because he no longer needed to stand on a rock to mount. He pressed his knees to Estrella's sides and galloped off, following Sky through the billowing snow.

"She needs water," Arriero said to Tijo before he could even slide from Estrella's back. "There's a stream over there. It's not far, but she's too weak to make it." Tijo thought for a moment. He had a skin bag made from the bladder of a long-horned sheep that had been slain for the spring festival. He used it to carry smaller bags of powders and potions. The bladder was not as good as the leather buckets used in the village for transporting water, but good enough. He emptied it and they rode to the nearby creek.

"This is a good creek," Estrella said over the vigorous gurgling. She paused and looked about some more. "We could make camp here. There's some wind protection from those rocks and the cottonwood on the other side. Yes, it's a good place, I think."

Tijo looked around as well. He was thrilled by Estrella's notion of a winter camp. The snow moons would be coming soon. And he thought of the bitter winds that would come and the marauding wolf storms on their tails.

As he filled the bladder with water, he recalled how angry the healer had been when the chieftain gave it to Haru at the spring festival. It had been her reward to her for curing the chieftain's wife. The healer had accused Haru of witchcraft, but the chieftain was at heart a sensible man, and so pleased to have his wife healthy again that he paid no attention to the healer's accusations.

Tijo was not sure how he could get the mare to drink. She lay on the ground in a nearly lifeless heap. Her breath was shallow and there seemed to be long periods when she drew no breaths at all. It reminded Tijo of Haru's last dying gasps. He worried that the mare could not swallow if she was flat on the ground. He carried a small cup with him, one that Haru had made him when he was a baby. He poured some water into it.

Hold On had knelt down, supporting himself on his forelegs. "Bella," he said softly. "Bella. We are all here to help you. Can you smell this clean water? You need to drink." But she said nothing. Her eyes rolled back in her head. Her tongue was parched and hung out of her mouth, the color of stone. "Pour some in her mouth, Tijo." Hold On said. "It might help. Just a little."

Tijo did as Hold On suggested. Bella's eyelids flickered a bit. *But how can she swallow?* Tijo wondered before an idea struck him.

"Hold On, remember the reeds growing by the creek?"

"I didn't see them, but I heard the wind blowing through them."

"Take me back. I have to pick some."

By the time they returned, the rest of the herd had arrived and were gathered around Bella.

"This poor mare. To be treated so," Corazón muttered.

"I'm going to try and give her some water with this reed," Tijo said.

The horses watched the boy suck some water from the bladder with the hollow reed, then hold his fingertip to the end so it would not fall out. Very gently he slid the reed into Bella's half-open mouth. Keeping his thumb on the end nearest to him, he raised it just a bit and let a tiny amount of water leak into her mouth. He did not want her to choke, so he allowed only the smallest bit to flow.

Soon, the mare raised her head from the ground and blinked. Tijo stroked her gently between the ears. Hold On licked some dust from her face. The mare lay down her head again and shut her eyes, peaceful with the knowledge of the kindness of the herd.

There had been much talk in the recent days of pressing forward to get across the distant mountains before the worst of winter arrived. But Estrella skillfully began to show the rest of the herd reasons for staying on. She had discovered a warm spring where the ground was always free from snow and the fat grass grew quite thickly. Not only that, but there was a broad depression in the ground where the earth was soft and warm. They found it a good place to sleep, especially on the coldest nights, and began calling it the wallow. On another day, Estrella discovered a place where some strange bulbous root vegetables grew. She gnawed on one and found it to have a unique, almost sweet taste. She brought it back and dropped it on the ground in front of Angela, who blinked with surprise and shoved her ears forward.

"Bless my withers, it's a turnip!" She tossed her head and whinnied. "Corazón, come look!" Corazón trotted over quickly, along with Grullo and Bobtail. The four horses looked in wonder at the bulging pale root that Estrella had found.

"A turnip!" Arriero said, his voice full of wonder and delight.

By this time Sky had arrived. "What's a turnip?"

"Oh, my," Corazón said almost mournfully. "The young'uns don't even know about turnips."

Hold On trotted toward them. "I smelled it from all the way over there. I can hardly believe it. I haven't had a turnip since the Old Land. The masters gave them to us as special treats, you know."

Estrella didn't know about the masters' special treats, but

she felt there was something very good about this root. "Well, I found it just past where the fat grass grows."

"You don't say," Grullo replied slowly. "You know, we might think about making this our winter camp. We've got good water, fat grass, and now turnips."

"That's exactly what I was thinking," Arriero said. Estrella was thrilled that it was Grullo who said this and not her. She had planted the seed for this idea, but now the herd was imagining it to be their own.

And so they stayed at this camp. Soon, Bella was well enough to walk to the creek and drink from the stream herself, and eat the fat grass that grew on its banks. She never spoke much, but they knew she was grateful.

On clear days, if they looked to the north, they could just make out an immense mountain range. It would be impossible for them to cross the mountains in the winter. It seemed sensible to wait until spring, but some of the horses wanted to go now and at least get closer to the foothills.

Tijo, however, doubted if anything closer to those mountains would make a good winter camp. There was fresh water here. There was plenty of fat grass that wintered well. There was small game. Tijo had ridden Bobtail and Arriero out two days in a row and brought back several grouse and a chicken partridge. He had also brought down four or five rabbits. Their white fur was thick and he had enough pelt to make himself a hood.

He had gone back to the tree and fetched the bobcat skin he had hung on the limb. He needed time, though, to dress all of these skins properly, wash them, stretch them, cure them. It was odd. Tijo was now well fed and would soon be warm in the furs of the bobcat. These were his human needs and yet he felt keenly the needs of the horses as well. He longed for the scent of the sweet grass as much as they did. His life, his fate had become inextricably entwined with theirs.

Every night, the horses gathered in the wallow to make the weather shelter. It seemed like a special place — a place where winter could not come even though it might be snowing furiously. A place where the wind grew calm and came with a sigh rather than a bluster across the vast plains. A place where the moonlight trickled down through the leafless branches of a tree until one could almost imagine the buds of spring.

One evening, Tijo could not sleep. Estrella was on guard at the edge of the wallow, so he got up and made his way carefully around the large bodies of the horses that surrounded him.

Estrella could tell that something was troubling him. She lowered her head and tousled his hair with her muzzle. "What's wrong?"

Tijo turned and looked at the filly for a long time before answering. "Have you ever seen something that maybe at first you think is not real but then begin to believe it?"

Estrella felt a tremor pass through her. She nodded but was reluctant to say anything. Not yet at least. It had been so long since she had seen the flickering tiny horse that had guided them so faithfully.

"Tell me, Tijo." She neighed so softly he could barely hear it. "What is it that you have seen?"

He was silent a long while. "I've seen an owl — an *omo* owl, the people call it. It has a white face and flies very silently through the night. And I think this owl is perhaps the spirit lodge for Haru, the woman who raised me."

"Spirit lodge?"

"Yes. In the world of our people, some spirits become guardians for those they left behind. They take leave of the spirit camps from time to time to look in on those they have loved. Haru found me when I had been cast out to die because of my lame leg and now she follows me as I live. But lately she has not come so often and I think it is because I have you, the first herd." He paused. "Now it is your turn to tell me what you have seen."

Estrella threw her head back as far as she could. "You see the dipping cup stars and how the last one points?"

"Yes. The North Star."

"It is our guide star."

"But that star is real. No one would call you foolish for using the North Star as your guide star."

"I know, but I have another guide in my mind's eye," Estrella said.

She told him about the tiny horse she had first spied in the flash of her dam's eye as she was dying.

"It took me a long time to understand what this horse was, what it meant. I would see it carved in the cliff rocks as if it had been there forever. And then one day I realized it *had* been there forever. I had thought I was leading the herd toward the sweet grass, but then I realized that this tiny horse was really leading us on a trail older than time, not just to the sweet grass but to . . . to . . ."

"To what?"

"To the place where horses began. You see, we are coming home to the place where we started. She is First Horse. The dawn horse."

Tijo reached up and put his hands on either side of Estrella's lovely face. He had grown so tall that it was easy for him to touch the star on her forehead, for which she had been named. He began to trace it with his finger.

"Estrella, I saw your tiny horse."

"What?" She almost staggered with astonishment. Had he looked so deep into her eyes when he stitched his own face that he had seen the constellations that swept the midnight of her mind?

"I saw it with the owl."

"The one you believe to be the spirit lodge for Haru?" Estrella asked.

Tijo nodded. "It was the oddest thing. That night when I first saw the *omo* owl, I felt as if my own spirit had slipped from my body, as if I were outside my own skin but looking at myself at the same time. Then the owl spoke."

"What did it say?"

"It spoke of many things, some I didn't understand. It spoke of something called *ga* that would only be known in times to come."

"Times to come?" Estrella was bewildered.

"And the *omo* owl told me the same thing you told me. 'First Horse,' it said. 'The dawn horse.' He is the one who leads the herd."

"But where is he now? And where is your *omo* owl?" Estrella asked, her voice tinged with sadness. She looked longingly into Tijo's eyes as if searching for the dawn horse but seeing only her own reflection.

"I think they are with us, Estrella. You and I might be what *omo* calls long spirits or weavers of time, but we are both of us threads in the same blanket." Tijo tipped his head back and looked up at the starry blanket of the night and pulled his own more tightly around his shoulders.

CHAPTER 17

Soundless Words

It was a starry night, and El Miedo was riding Pego through a territory thick with the scent of bobcat, yet the stallion did not shy. One of El Miedo's lieutenants wheeled his own horse about and began beating her savagely on the shoulder because the mare refused to go on.

"Ah! Don Roberto, your mare is stubborn." El Miedo snickered.

"There's blood ahead on the trail. It must be bobcat blood; that is the only thing that makes this mare shy."

"Ride beside me. El Noble is steady."

"The stallion doesn't shy?"

"Never!" El Miedo said smugly.

From the corner of his eye, Pego saw the slinking shadow of

Coyote. This was his moment. He sensed it. *Your night to be named. Your proper name to come from the heavens,* the familiar voice whispered in his head.

The mare named Artemisia pranced nervously beside the stallion.

"There's blood down the trail ahead. Bobcat blood," she neighed.

"Artemisia, you are named for the hunting goddess. And you let a little blood scare you," Pego replied.

"A bobcat killed my foal and you expect me not to be frightened?"

He snorted in disdain. "I expect you to do your duty. To serve!"

"And you are not frightened?"

"As my master said — never!"

Pego began to trot forward. His master gave him his head, as the stallion was fearless and seemed to know where he should go. He came to a quick halt near the blood, dropped his muzzle, sniffing the ground. He had picked up another scent. Not quite horse but almost. Was it ... horse ... horse and perhaps human? The scent of three creatures' blood threaded in the air. And then El Miedo spied the droppings. He dismounted to examine the droppings and the tracks. Two minutes later, he came racing back to El Noble.

"Horses have come this way!" El Miedo exclaimed. He gave the stallion a pat, then looked at the sky. The winged horse constellation glittered fiercely. "*¡Dios mío!* The stars shine their light on this horse."

It was as the dream foretold. The kingdom, the crown, an empire were about to be his. He had found the trail of horses.

"El Noble found the trail," the lieutenant exclaimed. "We will capture those horses and then we go on and capture the land."

"El Noble is no longer his name," El Miedo retorted. "From here on, he shall be called by the name of the heavenly winged horse of the night. We shall call him Pegasus. Summon the priest."

Pego's heart thundered in his chest. *Vengeance and ascendance.* Coyote's words rang in his head. He turned his head to a slope encrusted with sagebrush and watched the coyote dance off into the night.

The plump padre came riding up from the rear ranks. He dismounted his horse with the help of a groom and hurried up to where El Miedo stood beside his stallion. The two men exchanged words briefly. The padre sent the groom back to fetch his saddlebag. When he returned, the padre took out a vial of holy water and a white cloth that he used to bless the horses on Saint Eligius Day. However, that was a blessing, not a christening. Could a beast be christened? And to christen that animal with the name of a heathen god — Pegasus? He was unsure, though he dared not question El Miedo. But what would His Holiness say? Well, His Holiness was far, far away. The padre nodded at El Miedo, who flicked his whip lightly behind Pego's knee. Pego lowered his head and bent his knee until it was flat on the ground. His opposite leg extended in a graceful forward slant. El Miedo nodded once again to the padre, who began to sprinkle holy water on Pego's head.

"May this horse, O Lord, receive thy blessing and be sound in body and by the grace of Saint Anthony, the patron of all animals, be preserved from evil. I christen you Pegasus in the name of the Father, the Son, and the Holy Ghost. Amen."

Pego felt the little droplets of water on his head and shoved his ears forward as the priest's muttering rolled over him. *Was there ever such a horse as I?* he thought, and felt a thrill course through his veins.

The weather grew colder, but that only made Tijo work harder and faster to cure the bobcat skin. He washed the bobcat's hide along with those of the rabbits, too.

"How long will this take?" Bobtail asked. He had never really come around to the idea of remaining at this camp for the winter.

"Well, it takes a few days to really cure a hide properly."

Estrella caught Bobtail and Arriero exchanging glances. Had Bobtail convinced Arriero as well?

"I never thought I would want hands," Corazón said. "Look how red that poor boy's hands are from the freezing water. Can't you use the water from the warm springs?"

"No. That water is not good for drinking or for washing hides."

"It's only going to get colder," Bobtail said. "The sooner we get to the sweet grass, the better it will be for all of us."

"Not all of us." Estrella whinnied and looked toward Bella.

"You can leave me," Bella said. "I am getting a bit better each day now. I'll catch up if you go on."

"No, Bella," Estrella said firmly.

"But if she says she'll catch up . . ." Bobtail snorted.

"None of us is going to catch up with anything before those mountains, and the one place you do not want to be when winter strikes is in the mountains," Hold On said. He paused and looked toward Estrella, then flicked his ears.

Estrella knew she must be firm about this. "The sweet grass is not before the mountains. It's on the other side. That much I can tell you. Even if Bella were not with us, it is too big a risk to travel now." She paused, then added, "But you are free to go if that is truly what you want to do."

The words hung in the air like suspended ice crystals. There was a long silence. Angela now stepped toward Tijo and gave his red hands a warming lick with her tongue.

"I wish we could help, dear." She chuckled. "Silly me, if

only we did have hands like Corazón said." The tension suddenly broke.

"You can help," Tijo said as a thought struck him. He had
gathered only enough alder limbs to build a stretching frame
for the bobcat's skin but not for the rabbits'. "I've seen you pick
up branches and chew the bark right off a tree. I need branches
like those over there in the pile. Can you get me some and strip
them for me?"

Grullo walked over to the pile and examined the neatly
stacked slender limbs that Tijo had stripped of their bark.

"We can do this," he said. "Just have to get a good grip with
your cheek teeth and bite. A single snap, I think, and the
branch will break."

The horses were excited, and it didn't take long before the
pile of alder branches had doubled. Tijo had more than enough
for his stretching racks. The horses stood back and watched
him intently as he bound together the racks with the gut of the
bobcat, which he had saved, and set them firmly in the ground.
There was hardly a part of the animals that he did not use. The
intestines he had removed, cleaned, dried, then cut into thin
strips. The tendons he had carefully separated from the muscles. Before he put the skin on the stretcher, he had taken his
curved stone hand blade, which looked as if it had been made
to fit his palm, and began scraping away the flesh and fat.
Then, to the horses' shock, he cracked open the skull of the

bobcat, scooped out the brains, and began to spread them on the scraped skins, adding creek water as he mashed the mixture into the skin.

"Why are you doing that?" Sky asked, lowering his head very close to the skin.

"It makes the hide very soft, soft to sleep under. Soft to wear."

"When do you put it on the stretcher?" Estrella asked.

"Not until tomorrow."

The horses stuck out their necks and shoved their ears forward.

"Huh?" Grullo snorted.

Tijo suddenly realized he had spoken in the language of his people, something he hadn't done since he had started traveling with the herd. He was not sure what language he used to communicate with the horses, as it was not exactly spoken, and yet they heard each other, could listen and understand one another.

"What did you just say?" Estrella asked.

"I am sorry. I slipped back into the old tongue, the tongue of my people. Haru always told me to do this when we worked on skins. She said let the brains sleep with the skin, let the skin sleep with the brains, and soft dreams shall be your blessing."

The skins were finished just in time for the first blizzard. Tijo sat with the bobcat fur draped over his shoulders. He wore a rabbit hood on his head that he had just stitched up, and was now completing a muffler from the other rabbit skin.

"You look like an animal!" Sky exclaimed.

"A funny sort of creature," Verdad said. "Part cat, part rabbit."

"I feel warm. I don't care what I look like," he said, glancing up at his friends. "But I have one more skin I want to get. A big buck."

"Buck?" Estrella asked.

"A deer, you know. A buck or a doe," Tijo replied. "A doe would be nice."

Hold On stepped forward. "Why? Why would you need a deer?" His voice trembled. The other horses had fallen silent. "Their fur is not thick."

"Their skins." He plucked at his trousers. "For clothes. Haru made these for me and now, look, I have nearly outgrown them. And their antlers. I can make knives from them, and then of course eat their meat."

There was an almost deathly silence. Tijo could feel the horses withdrawing from him, sliding away as they stood there perfectly still. "What's wrong? I don't understand."

Estrella had retreated to some unknowable place. She stared at him blankly but in her mind's eye she saw bones, the bones of a young fawn. She saw the marks of the big mountain lions' claws on its ribs as they had torn the fawn apart to get at its heart, and then she saw the fawn's skull and the scratches of a coyote's teeth that had picked the skull clean after the cats had had their fill of the meat.

Estrella stepped forward. "Tijo, we know you need meat, but you cannot eat the deer — not the buck, nor the doe, nor a fawn."

The single word *fawn* made the horses lay their ears flat.

Tijo was shocked. They had never shown such a fearful response to him. But he made no mistake — it was him they feared. The thought that he had somehow frightened these lovely creatures sickened him. "What have I done?"

"Nothing yet," Angela said. "But you cannot kill a deer." She took a deep breath. "You see, deer, like ourselves, are grazers. It would be like killing our own. We are too close to deer."

Estrella came closer to him. Very close. She was almost whispering, for what she said seemed to be only for Tijo. The others sensed this and backed a bit away.

"Remember, Tijo, what you told me, that we are long spirits, time weavers, and how our spirits stretch into the deep past? You said we we are all . . ."

"All threads in the same blanket."

"Yes, threads in the same blanket. The deer are part of this blanket. They look different from us, the way the tiny horse looks different. But once, there were not so many differences and we were alike — one herd."

"One herd," Tijo repeated. Then he stood up. He looked at the horses and began to speak. He hoped his words would not fall into the gulf now between them. "I am sorry. I have given offense. Hold On spoke of the things you had to forget. I, too, must forget many things. I shall forget hunting deer. I shall forget the deer dances my people did in the autumn. I shall make my trousers from the skins of other animals. I shall never eat the meat of a deer or use its antlers to make a knife or tools. But what I shall not forget is your history, your time on this earth from the very beginnings. For I now understand that you are coming home and I . . . I am just a newcomer to this land where you started."

As he spoke, Tijo felt the gulf between them contract. He saw a new brightness in their eyes that minutes before had turned dull and empty and stared out at him as if from skulls. Their ears relaxed and began to turn this way and that to catch the often soundless words in the mysterious language that he and the horses shared.

CHAPTER 18

The Ravine

God has blessed this expedition, El Miedo thought. Since Pego had found the horses' trail, the winds had blown the scent toward them. Horses were the key to the empire he dreamed of relentlessly. At first he had been nervous when the dream creature in the form of Coyote had visited. He thought he was the devil! But now he knew that the *perro zorro* was a blessing, like the stallion. "Twiced blessed I am," El Miedo said to himself.

Once he had these new horses, he would carry out the strategy he had been devising for months. He planned to swing west and south so he could meet up with the Seeker, then vanquish him and his puny following. The Seeker had only a fraction of the horses that El Miedo commanded, and a straggly herd of men, the dregs of the Iber fighting forces. Half of them were actually farm laborers or louts he had picked up from bars in the small northern villages of the Old Land. They were not disciplined. They did not know horses, not the way he did. El Miedo had his spies. They reported back to him. Once he got these horses, he was confident he could make short work of the man called the Seeker and make the New World his own. The wind blew harder. The acrid scent of the horses' sweat filled his nostrils. *And with this wind,* thought El Miedo, *I am thrice blessed. Yes, even the wind is on my side. God is on my side and the wind as well!*

Had the wind been in the opposite direction, the herd might have caught *their* scent. El Miedo had left behind the carts, the mules, and had set out on the trail with his best men on their best horses. It was the elite legion. *La Legión de su Majestad la Reina,* the Legion of Her Majesty the Queen. It was near sunset on the second day when a sudden cloud of dust rose up from the horizon. Horses!

El Miedo signaled to his two senior lieutenants. It was time to put the plan into effect. *El Bolsillo,* he called the plan, or the Pocket. As the legion spread out into the configuration of *el Bolsillo,* they accelerated their pace. "We are about to pull the drawstrings of the pocket," El Miedo murmured to Pego.

The horses would put up a fight, no doubt, but they were no match for El Miedo. He would catch them and break them, break them as he broke everything that stood in his way.

The horses of the first herd had been traveling just beyond the usual boundaries of their winter camp. The last few days had been warm and snowbanks had melted away, so they had gone out to forage for grass. The wind shifted. A different scent — not the fresh new green of spring and sun but of sweat — sweat from the footpads of a coyote. Like a current from a dreadful tributary, the odor coursed through, fouling the green river of grass. Hold On stopped grazing and jerked his head.

"What's wrong?" Tijo asked. He was astride the stallion's back and lost in his own daydreams.

"Coyote!" Hold On replied. "They sweat from their feet like dogs. A coyote has been this way."

"Coyote? Are you sure?" Hold On felt Tijo stiffen and grip his sides.

Estrella gave a sharp snort seconds later. "I smell something! Coyote! Let's turn a bit. There's grass west of the camp where I scouted yesterday."

"I agree," Hold On replied. "Nothing good comes from crossing a coyote's territory."

Estrella flinched. She knew this better than any of them.

They turned and Estrella accelerated their pace from the leisurely trot to a gallop, not full out but what the horses called "close on," packed tightly yet moving swiftly.

Not much time had passed before they picked up the scent again. *This is odd,* Estrella thought. *How can a coyote cover that much ground so quickly?* It was the same coyote. Of this she was sure. She could tell by the scent. Once more she signaled a turn, with two sharp snorts. And again they picked up the scent. But the wind shifted and another overwhelming scent came upon them. It was salty, but not like the fresh salt smell of the sea. And not the smell that leaked from the coyote's footpads. It was the rotten salt odor of sweat through skin, human skin.

"Men!" Estrella's whinny was high-pitched and frantic. "Men on horses!"

Corazón and Angela froze in their tracks. They turned to each other with looks of disbelief. Disbelief and despair, as if they were too old for what was coming, too tired to run. The terrified squeals of Verdad and Sky split the air. The first herd broke into a full-flight gallop, their necks stretched out as they raced across the plain.

Estrella dared not look back. She felt the energy of the herd behind her, streaming through her. The earth trembled with the pounding of their hooves. Their own sweat now spun off like white strings into the sunlit air. The clouds seemed to stand still in the sky while the ground beneath their hooves blurred. But their was no joy in this gallop. They were running for their very lives.

Pego could feel El Miedo's tension. He also felt the spurs dig into his flanks. *If I am a god, why does he jab me with his spurs?* He faltered slightly and the spurs dug in deeper. No time to think, but he knew that blood had been drawn. He pressed forward harder. He would show this man who rode him. He quickly was gaining ground. They were closing in on the haunches of two old mares who had fallen behind.

"*¡Adelante! ¡Adelante!* El Noble. *¡Mi Pego!*" El Miedo urged.

But it is the filly we want. Not the old mares! Pego thought. Still, he felt El Miedo picking up the lariat looped around the saddle horn. Seconds later he heard the hissing sound of it swirling over his head. It soared into the air, inscribing the sky with a perfect circle that began to fall over the mare's head, the one called Corazón. A terrible shriek rent the air, not from Corazón, but Angela.

Tijo turned around and felt a cold blade of fear stab him. The mare was struggling to keep galloping, but the rope had tightened. Her neck twisted at an odd angle and within seconds she was down, flailing on the ground.

Estrella galloped up beside them, matching her stride to Hold On's.

"Quick, onto my back, Tijo," she ordered.

"What is it?" Hold On asked as he felt Tijo leap from him.

"Corazón. She's down. You keep galloping," Tijo replied. "Estrella and I will go back for her."

"But ropes. If they have her with ropes, how will you get her?"

Estrella was determined that no horse be left behind, abandoned to the mercies of the Ibers. This was what it meant to lead — to protect every member of your herd even if you had to risk your own life. She was one with the herd and inseparable.

El Miedo blinked. He saw a horse. The strong young filly whose scent he had caught was bolting toward the lariat with a rider on her back. *If only I had two ropes!* El Miedo thought. But there were more men with ropes behind him closing in. What he saw next was inconceivable. The filly with the rider was charging straight for the old mare. The boy reached down and with one swift motion severed the rope with his hunting knife. The mare was free, back on her feet and streaking ahead.

Estrella could hear the pounding heart of the old mare racing beside her.

"You can do it, Corazón. Remember your big heart." And Corazón knew she could do it. *I can! I can! I . . . I . . .* Then she heard Estrella gasp. And Tijo shrieked, "No!"

A deep ravine loomed ahead. That was where the coyote had been driving them. *Coyote!* Estrella thought. How had he tricked them this time? She felt something flicker from deep within her, or was it outside of her? The tiny star horse glittered in her mind's eye.

It was like during the fire, when the tiny star horse had appeared to her out of the smoke and flames so she could lead the others out of the canyon. But at that time, it had been only herself who had seen the tiny horse. Now it seemed as if the horse was alive in all of their minds, like the earliest star rising in the twilight before the coming darkness of the night.

Estrella was the first to fly off the edge of the ravine. Tijo turned around to shout to Hold On, "You can do it, Old Fellow. You can do it!"

But there was no need for words. The image of the tiny horse sparkled in the old stallion's blind eyes. He felt the force of his legs as he broke into a tremendous leap and sailed across the ravine. The other horses followed. Estrella spied the first of the evening stars rising in the dusky night. A wild whinny curled into the air. "Jump for the stars." It was a jubilant sound. First herd leapt, and it did seem as if the stars embraced them as they arced over the ravine.

El Miedo on Pego screeched to a halt as his dream began to vanish. He jabbed his spurs into Pego's flanks, gouging him again and again until blood poured down the stallion's legs. He began cursing him.

"You dumb, stupid, cowardly beast. You are no better than a plow animal, a mule. Stupid mule. You have betrayed me!"

But all Pego could think was that Coyote had betrayed them. He reared up suddenly and then changed ends and started bucking madly. El Miedo, still screeching, knew he must hang on. If he fell off, the horse would trample him to death. El Miedo vowed that he would kill this horse before he was thrown. He pulled out the Crusader dagger from Toledo and was about to drive it into Pego's neck, when suddenly he felt himself losing his grip and being flung to the ground.

This must be the end, he thought, and steeled himself for the crushing weight of the horse's hoof on his skull. But he was shocked. The horse Pego was standing perfectly still, his gaze fixed on something across the ravine. El Miedo turned his head to look. On the opposite side of the ravine, at its very edge, was a fine-looking bay mare.

"Bella!" Pego whinnied. "Bella!"

The mare turned and cantered off. Pego then began to walk toward El Miedo. The man rose to his knees and put his hands together as if in prayer.

"*Por favor . . . mi amigo noble . . .*" But Pego tossed his head, then reared and, spinning around in the opposite direction, galloped off. El Miedo remained stunned on his knees as the dusk gathered around him. He watched the sun slip low, spreading across the horizon like the yolk of a bloodied egg.

CHAPTER 19

First Angry

Coyote burrowed deeper in his den. He had run off when the chase went awry. He was furious. He wanted to be rid of men and of horses. He was sick of other creatures' dreams. He had done his part, rounded up the herd, driven them toward the ravine. Who knew they would dare to leap? He thought he was rid of them, of all horses.

But now these creatures had invaded his new territory, and that strange boy was snatching his prey! Sage grouse and every other ground bird that he feasted on through the long winter. First Angry he was called. But now, as he often thought, the name did not quite fit, for he was too clever, too clever to allow anger to get in the way of his cunning. A familiar sound pulled him from his poisonous thoughts. Hoofbeats. He came closer to the opening of his den and peered out.

An immense shimmering moon had risen. He blinked, for a strange design was printed against its silver surface, an odd assemblage of things both human and animal. A twisted creature like a two-headed beast with the boy on top and his spear a slash across the moon. He blinked again. The heads seemed to separate and now he could see more clearly. It was two horses. The old blind stallion and the young filly.

Well, they wouldn't find him. There had been a snowfall and he had covered his tracks, using his tail to brush his paw prints away. He blessed the coyote god for giving him such a fine bushy tail. He had also laid a false track, a scent trail with the remains of a doe he had brought down days before. But his anger still simmered as he watched them. *Don't be angry,* he chided himself. *Be clever. Be cunning. For that is what you are — the dream stealer, the fantastic concealer. Crafty and sly, I'll sell you lies.* He had spun a snare of lies around him now so they would never find him.

Hold On stopped and peeled back his lips. He was picking up a scent. At first, they had objected to Hold On coming. But now they understood why he had insisted. As Corazón had said, "It's as if that stallion has eyes in his nose!" The stallion gave a barely discernible nod of his head and flicked his ears toward a small knoll. The snow seemed unbroken by any animal. There was no visible trail, only snowy humps that suggested a buried stump or shrub. They moved slowly in the direction Hold On had indicated. Soon they picked up the odor. It was peculiar. *Deer but not deer,* Estrella thought. And Tijo leaned down closer to examine the snow. There was something odd about it. The snow did not seem as if it had fallen here but rather had been blown or brushed. A bitter wind was blowing down on them, so cold that it caused Tijo's eyes to water. He wiped away the tears and felt the bump of the bobcat scar on his cheek. It suddenly seemed to burn. How could he be so cold and the scar feel as if it were burning? He drew the rabbit fur hood tighter around his head.

Coyote could not believe it. In his den he heard the crunching sound of the snow the hooves made as the horses approached. *They're coming! Coming here! How did they find me?* Coyote's guard hairs stood straight out as he chanted to himself — *I am the trickster! I am the trickster!*

The horses shied as Coyote exploded from the burrow and leapt into the night. Coyote, who had led them nearly into the hands of the men! They had not expected this direct, bold attack from a creature known for his cunning. The savage barks splintered the night. He was the essence of cruelty, vicious and meaningless cruelty. He sank his teeth into Hold On's front leg. Hold On screamed and, with his powerful hind legs, reared into the air. The coyote hung on. They were an odd, entangled form writhing in the moonlight. Then Hold On's feet began to slip. He was on the ground on his back. A stain of blood blossomed on the snow. Estrella felt Tijo slip from her back, not fall but slip off on purpose. With his dagger in one hand and his spear in the other, Tijo ran around the tangled, kicking stallion, trying to get a clear shot at Coyote and not accidentally stab Hold On. But they were wrestling on the ground in a hopeless snarl of limbs like some demonic flower, its petals tinted in blood, blooming in the winter night. Raw, desperate cries scratched the cold wind, which began to blow harder.

Estrella and Tijo knew they could not let Coyote get to Hold On's neck and sink his fangs into the life-giving artery. Suddenly, there was a tearing sound overhead, a high-pitched *shreeeeee*. A white face hung in the night, then, folding its wings, sliced down through the darkness, its face like a hurtling moon. Coyote yowled in rage. Tijo and Estrella looked up in amazement as the owl, with Coyote in its talons, rose in the night. Hold On had staggered to his feet. His wounds were not serious.

However, Coyote was still howling with rage. The shadow of the owl and the witch dog spread out over the snowscape and then the owl rose higher over the crown of the trees. The branches of those trees murmured in the wind. Tijo, Estrella, and Hold On all tipped their heads toward the sky. The yips and barks of Coyote grew fainter. Suddenly, the *omo* owl released Coyote. He came blistering through the night straight down like a yellow comet, hitting the ground a few feet from the two horses and the boy, broken but still gasping.

The horses and the boy approached and hung over him. The creature was attempting to speak, although his body seemed completely mangled and askew.

"Tricked," he gasped. That was his last word. Tijo took his dagger and stabbed him in the heart. The eyes of Coyote froze in shock. But beneath the glaze of death, there lurked the last remnants of a powerful anger.

They returned to the camp and once more the horses gathered around to watch Tijo with his needle close up the torn flesh of Hold On. Luckily, although Coyote's fangs had come close to a tendon, it was not close enough to cut it. The bleeding had almost stopped by the time they were back. Not many stitches were required, not nearly as many as Estrella's shoulder wound had. After stitching up the wound, Tijo made a cleansing poultice of devil's claw and hemp and bound the leaves tightly to Hold On's leg. When he had completed tending Hold On, he turned his attention to the dead coyote. He would take his hide and cure it well.

He worked carefully on the skin. It was very important that he do every step just right, with no excessive cuts. Except for removing the brains from the skull, he wanted to keep the head as intact as possible. He would not use this as a blanket. He had no desire to sleep under the skin of this conniving animal. Instead, it would serve as a totem to fend off evil, a spirit chaser.

Slivers of light began to lengthen the days and from a distance the horses and the boy could hear what they called white thunder, slides of snow hurtling down steep slopes.

"That's where we are heading," Estrella said one morning as she, with Tijo on her back and Hold On by their side, looked north. The earth was unlocking as spring approached and new smells were unleashed into the morning air. Tijo could see both Estrella and Hold On peeling back their lips to catch these new scents.

"Do you smell the sweet grass yet?"

Estrella shook her head. "That is not the sweet grass. That smells different."

"I know what it is," Tijo replied.

"Really?" Hold On asked. "What?"

"A creature — a grazing creature but not a deer. Much bigger." He thought a minute. "An animal so huge it sounds like thunder when it runs. It has shaggy long fur. And a head so big, almost as big as I stand tall!" Tijo was very proud of how tall he had grown.

"Have you really seen this creature?" Hold On asked.

"No, but I have slept under its skin."

"How? Where is the skin now?"

"It is a long story." Tijo hesitated.

"A snow story?" Estrella asked. For on the coldest blustery nights when blizzards struck and engulfed the landscape, the horses loved to tell stories.

"Yes — a snow story. So we'll wait until next winter."

Tijo had not revealed much of his past. He knew the horses, especially Estrella, were curious.

Hold On lifted his head a bit. "I am not sure if you will have to wait that long. I smell a storm coming. A late winter storm — almost spring storm. They can be fierce."

By dusk a few flakes had begun to fall. Tijo had built a small fire to cook the fish he had caught in the stream. None of the other horses were about. They were away, foraging for the last bits of vegetation before their favorite spots, which had melted out just a few days ago, were covered again.

"Tijo," Estrella began, "you say we are long spirits that have stretched deep into the past. That you and I are threads in the same blanket." Tijo nodded. He sensed what was coming. "I have told you of my time on the ship. Of my memories of my dam. Of the shark that killed her. Of the island where we first swam to. Of the City of the Gods, where we were captured. But you have told me nothing really about yourself from the time before . . . before you and Hold On found each other. I want to know. We became a herd, I mean really became a herd, on the night of our first blizzard in this new world. That was when we told our stories. It is time for you to tell yours. You are already a part of this herd. Can't you trust us with your stories? The stories, the ones of the thunder creature, or how you came to learn medicine and why you left the people — can you not tell us those stories?"

CHAPTER 20

The Blanket Stories

By the time the herd gathered around Tijo, the snow had begun to fall hard. The small fire glowed, enveloping the horses and the boy in a pale orange cocoon of light. The bobcat-skin blanket was wrapped tightly around him, and he'd pulled the rabbit hood down so low and the muffler of a rabbit so high that only a narrow slot revealed his eyes and mouth.

"There have been many blankets in my life." Tijo began speaking slowly. "But I came naked into the world and, hours after I was born, was left naked at the edge of the old meat trail that the people followed to hunt." The horses snorted in dismay. "Yes, I was to be meat, prey for other creatures. You see" — he pulled out his leg from the coverings — "I was cursed. This crooked leg. So they wanted to get me and my mother out from the clan. My mother died minutes after she gave birth to me. So they set me out on the meat trail, a run for coyotes, wolves, and mountain cats.

"Luckily, Haru found me quickly, just before a coyote was ready to attack, and no animals had eaten at me. However, I was very still and very blue from the cold. So she took off her own blanket to wrap me in. It was buckskin on one side and fleece on the other. That was my first blanket. She wrapped me tight in it and blew breath into my mouth. She said within seconds my lips began to turn pink. She picked me up and brought me home, home to her lodge. She lived somewhat apart from her own clan, the People of the Burnt River, and she kept my existence a secret. If someone heard me crying when they came to her for medicine, she told them she had found a baby lamb and was nursing it with ewe's milk.

"It was only necessary to keep the secret for one moon. If after a moon a cursed baby is still alive, it cannot be cast out. When the healer found out about me, he was very angry. But the chieftain refused to hear his complaints. After all, Haru's medicine had saved his wife. To celebrate my one month of life, Haru made me a blanket. That was the custom of our people. If a baby survives for one month, a naming blanket is woven for it. The blanket had the river design that is a symbol of our clan, and also the symbol for my name, Tijo, which means 'treasure found.' It was particularly special because it contained the hair of a thunder creature. The hide of that huge beast, when spread out flat, covered the entire floor of our lodge. In winter, there was nothing warmer."

"How did she come upon the pelt of the thunder creature?" Estrella asked.

"Haru's mate had brought the creature down, but he was killed in the hunt. Still, the blanket was his, for it was his spear that pierced the hide.

"The healer was furious. A white creature like that was thought to have powerful magic and now it belonged to Haru, of whom he was already jealous because of her medical skills. The healer tried to bring the matter before the clan council, but the chief refused to hear the case. The healer was so desperate, he even tried to take Haru for a wife. She said 'never.' Haru told me it took her three months to skin and tan the pelt of the thunder creature, but it was the most beautiful pelt rug you have ever seen.

"For my five-year blanket, she wove in some more threads of the thunder creature. That animal's pelt was so thick you would never be able to tell she had taken any. In fact, Haru would joke that the thunder creature grew the hairs back as soon as she removed them. I sometimes think the hair of the thunder creature helped me grow and become stronger in spite of my crooked leg. Haru always said perfect is boring and it can be mistakes, flaws, that make us strong and interesting. A little more than a year before Haru died, a baby was born with a caul on his head."

"A caul?" Sky asked.

"That happens sometimes with foals," Corazón said. "Yes. It's just part of the birth sac. It slips off easily enough or one can nip it off. There is no harm."

"No harm at all." Tijo nodded. "Just the opposite. The people say these infants are lucky and so this one was named Toshi 'N Tuki, or Boy Born with Luck on His Head. Haru was called to snip away the cap. Usually, they bind it with some sheep fleece or maybe a hair from a badger. But Haru especially liked this baby's mother, so she bound it up with a white hair from the thunder creature's pelt and then Haru, with the mother, would bury it. She felt it might bring extra good luck to Tuki. Tuki, that is what we called him. And I think it did bring him luck. He learned how to crawl very early, then toddle, and was saying lots of words before his first birthday. He's a very smart baby. And kind. I knew he wouldn't tease me like the other kids often did. They called me Lame Boy."

"Lame Boy?" Yazz shook her head. "It's as if all they saw was your leg and not the rest of you."

Tijo sighed. "They didn't see the rest of me. Not like Haru did. The healer had many wives and many children. His children would tease me mercilessly. He had one son a year or so older than me who was a big bully. Hikyu was his name. He was not that bright, but I swear the healer encouraged him to torture me." Tijo glanced at the coyote skin that he carried on his spear when he was not hunting. The spear was planted in the snow upwind of the fire.

"One time, Hikyu actually made a snare for me. I had gone up to the top of a hill where there was some grass that my old ewe loved. We were coming down the path and suddenly the ewe stopped. Her tail, which had been wagging a second before, froze and her ears flared out. 'Go on, go on,' I said, and prodded her with the staff. I had never had to use the staff before. But she would not budge. Then I heard it, a low chittering like hundreds of tiny beads being shaken in a small drum. The drum of course was the hole that had been artfully concealed with a mat of sage twigs and a few rocks. I made a wide circle around the spot so I could poke at the snare and dislodge the trip line. I knew about snares, as Haru had already begun teaching me how to make them. I poked. The ceiling of the snare fell through and there was the loud thrum of a dozen rattlesnakes squirming and rattling their tail rattles. But at the same moment, the ewe picked up another sound from behind a big clump of rabbitbrush. She charged. There was a scream as Hikyu tumbled out of the clump of rabbitbrush. He had set this snare for me.

"Haru was furious when she found out about this. And that was when the people began choosing sides. They knew the chieftain was old and might die. If he did, his son, who was weak and not very smart, would become the next chief of the Burnt River Clan. The healer would have more power, more influence. Or as Haru said, 'The real rattlesnakes shall be let loose.'

"And things did get worse. The bullying increased, but people still came to Haru when they were really sick and could not be cured by the healer. People from other clans even came to her.

"Then, maybe it was in this moon of a year ago, she began to feel sick. She said there was a numbness in her fingers and it began to spread. I knew she was dying and I knew one day she would go Otang."

"Go Otang?" Grullo asked.

"It is the way of the people. When they feel death is coming for them, they often decide to go out and meet it. But . . . but . . ." Tijo began to stammer. "I could not bear the thought of Haru dying alone. She had found me as an infant alone on the meat trail."

"She let you come?" Estrella asked.

Tijo waited a long time to reply. "There were conditions."

"Conditions?" Sky asked.

"Rules," Tijo replied. He began to speak and fell into the old tongue. None of the horses really understood him as he recalled the exact words Haru had used, but for Tijo it felt as if she were inhabiting his own body. Above them they heard the hoot of an owl, the *omo* owl, he thought, as he spoke the words that sounded so strange to the ears of the horses. "These are the rules: You do not speak. You do not bring me food. No water."

Then Tijo's voice shifted and the horses seemed to understand more as he continued.

"You do not make me warm by lying next to me or bringing me your star blanket. That blanket is for you. I wove that blanket for you. Not me. If the mountain lion comes, you go and let him eat me."

There was a long silence. Then Verdad asked, "Star blanket? Which one was that?"

"The last one she made me. My eleventh birthday would be coming and she must have known she would not live that long. So she made it and gave it to me early. The stars are made from many threads of the white thunder creature."

"But what happened to that thunder creature blanket, the one on the floor of your shelter from which she kept taking the threads for your blankets?" Sky asked.

"It was too heavy for me to bring when she set out on the way to Otang and she would not have permitted it. I imagine that when I did not come back, the healer took it along with all the other things in our lodge. He wanted so badly the magic he thought that blanket possessed."

"Did it have magic?" Sky asked.

Tijo shrugged. "If magic is love, to love something that has been cursed and said to bring bad luck, then yes, it had magic. If magic is to teach a boy with a crooked leg to throw a spear true and straight, then yes, it had magic. If magic is to teach a boy how to make the best snare ever, to say a prayer for a mother he never knew and know that in the first minutes of his life that person truly loved him as she had no other, then yes, it had magic. But I don't think any of that was magic. I think it was Haru. Just Haru."

CHAPTER 21

The Broken Thread

The winter snows had melted, but the spring rains had not come. The juniper leaves were curling tight and turning a sickly yellow. This was a sure sign of coming drought. Spring droughts were common, but following on the heels of a dry autumn, it would make it difficult for the people of the Burnt River Clan, and so they decided they would move even farther north than they had the year before. They would head toward the mountains, where there were signs of rain. Since Haru had died, the healer's power had increased as the chieftain had grown more frail. His appetite for power seemed boundless. Haru had seen this from the spirit camps and knew the time had come for her to return and seek a spirit lodge.

And so it was one evening when a deep purple thunderhead

languished in the dusk of a darkening sky that a white-faced owl, an *omo* owl, felt a soft jolt in its gizzard. *A spirit has lodged,* it thought, and began to fly toward the Yellow Cliffs. She could see that the pole sledges were being loaded for a departure at dawn the next morning. The Burnt River People had retired early so they would be ready. She perched on one of the ledges of the cliff dwellings. Nothing stirred in the camp. Their chieftain's sledge had been prepared. He would be unable to walk, so the thickest furs lined it, including the white pelt of the thunder creature. The spirit lodged in the *omo* owl took note. *So the healer has not claimed that yet!* But for some reason she was worried. Something made her anxious — if not the pelt itself, then something connected with it.

The openings in the cliff face, the doorways, reminded her of the dark vacant eyes of a skull. The owl felt a shiver pass through her flight feathers. She felt as if she were growing and stretching longer. *Wilfing,* a voice said. *That is what we call it. You have wilfed. You are as thin as the shadow of a reed.* It was Haru's host speaking to her. It was the *omo* owl. *The healer won't see you. Don't worry.* And in that moment the healer walked right by her.

Him!

Yes, him!

Haru suddenly felt a deep rustling. Her wings were spreading. A light breeze quivered at the edges of the flight feathers.

She flapped both wings. A puffy billow of air formed beneath them and Haru felt herself lifting into the air, into flight!

It was a dark, moonless night, but she was startled by the clarity of her vision. Not only her vision but her hearing. She could hear the heartbeat of the healer. Every breath he pulled into his lungs and then exhaled was like a wind blowing through a canyon. He was muttering, too. She heard her own name. "Haru . . . Haru . . . buried it . . ."

She suddenly knew where he was going. He wanted the thread of the pelt from the thunder creature. Tuki's mother must have brought the caul with her and hidden it along the way in various places as they made their journey. She dared not keep it. The healer must have followed her. But why did he need that thread? The chieftain would die soon and the healer could claim the whole blanket of the thunder creature. Why? Why?

The healer went directly to a tree that had been struck by lightning. It made sense that Tuki's mother had hidden it there because burnt wood usually was considered unlucky, but a totem of ill fortune when linked to something good was made impotent. The bad was canceled and even more good could come. In the case of charred wood, some said even a seedling could sprout from it. This could be a sign that the clan was entering fertile country. Then Haru, with the sharp eyes of the *omo* owl, spotted a quiver of bright green. A seedling poked from the charred wood. The drought must have ended here, and within the short time the clan had been camped here, there was evidence of renewal. Goodness had prevailed. *But not for long!* Haru felt something tremble within her. She knew it was the gizzard of her host, the *omo* owl.

The owl settled into the high branches of a nearby tree and observed. The healer stared for a moment at the seedling, then chuckled. A hunger for power, power in its most naked form, flooded through him. He took out his long, thin knife and cut off the seedling. The *omo* owl felt a sharp twinge now in its gizzard. Haru felt as if something in herself had been cut. *But I am a spirit. I cannot bleed,* Haru thought. Then she realized finally! *How did I not know this before? He is not just a healer but a witch.* But what kind of curse was he putting on the caul? She saw him begin to dig with his knife. He would not have to dig far to find it. There would be little left of the caul, but the thread from the thunder creature was all he wanted. She blinked and was again amazed by the sharpness of her sight.

She was right. There were just a few ragged remnants of the caul, but the pelt thread was still tied. Then the healer snipped the thread in two. He tucked the pieces into a small pouch that hung around his neck with the other amulets of a healer. She was sickened as she watched this.

When the healer returned to the camp of his people, he could not believe how quickly his luck turned. Within two days the chief would die! The whole blanket would be his. The luck from the boy born with the caul would begin to resettle and shift to him.

CHAPTER 22

When a Thread Breaks

The weather had turned so warm that the women of the Burnt River Clan had taken their clothes down to the stream to wash. The children were all playing in the shallow pools as their mothers worked. No one seemed to notice when Tuki, the Boy Born with Luck on His Head, wandered off. He was curious and began to follow a vole, and when he lost the trail of the vole, he found a partridge dragging its wing through the brush and felt sorry for the "poor birdie." He followed it out of the stand of trees, and then found himself on a high, wide-open plain. He turned to look for the stream where his mother was washing clothes, but there was no stream and there were no women and no children. What had happened? He didn't really know what a good little walker he was and how fast he had trotted off. For Toshi 'N Tuki, it was as if the world had walked away from him. They had forgotten him and left him alone in this vastness. He began to cry. "Ma Ma Mama!"

The setting sun glowered red and soon the sky swarmed with dark clouds. He felt as if the sky were scolding him. He heard a hiss like steam from his mother's boiling pot. Inches from him, a rattlesnake coiled up, ready to dart at his chubby leg. But before it could strike, a huge shadow engulfed him and there was a terrible shriek. A bird with wings as broad as Tuki was tall spiraled out of the air, its talons extended. The bird grasped the snake just behind its head and rose with it into the purpling sky. The snake writhed, slashing the air. The boy could still hear the awful racket of the rattles on its tail. Then suddenly the sound vanished. Something dropped from the sky. The boy stopped crying. He stared. A few feet in front of him lay the torn body of the dead snake. The huge bird lighted down.

"What to do with you?" the owl said. But the boy did not understand the owl's language. He merely stared at the white face of the bird.

"I want my mama." The *omo* owl did not have to understand the boy's language to know what he said. She walked up to him and spread her wings broadly around his shoulders and thought to herself, *He is too big to fly up to a hollow, but there must be a burrowing owl near here someplace, to keep him safe for the night.*

Tuki's father was furious. He stood across from the healer, scowling at his ridiculous talk of ghosts.

"You know boys born with cauls on the head attract ghosts," the healer said dismissively. "The ghost of the chieftain is still close. It frightened the boy away. We must go now. Escape from this haunted place."

"It's not true!" argued the father. "The boy has luck on his head."

"Give us one more day to look for him!" pleaded Tuki's mother.

"Are you challenging me?" The healer demanded, his voice low and dangerous. The clan looked on tensely. The very air between them seemed to crackle. Dry lightning forked in the sky, framing the healer, who stood tall and full of a hideous wrath, full of lies and lust for raw power.

"Yes, I am challenging you," the boy's father replied, and took out his knife. But the healer was quicker. A spurt of blood splashed in the night. The young father fell to the ground. The thin knife, the very one with which the healer had cut the seedling, quivered in his chest, its tip buried deep in the man's heart.

CHAPTER 23

An Unnerving Scent

At last the baby had stopped crying. Now he just whimpered. The burrowing owls had kept him safe during the night in their burrow, and the *omo* owl had brought him a fish that she had torn into small pieces for him to eat.

"I think the chick needs some berries," the female burrowing owl said. "I wish he'd eaten that snake. You tore it up into such nice little pieces for him."

"Maybe he's afraid that if he eats the snake meat, the rattles and the snake will come together again." The male burrowing owl fussed and brushed the baby's hair with his wing.

The Boy Born with Luck on His Head looked at the three owls gathered around him. The burrowing owls, a male and a female, had bright yellow eyes and a curve of bright white feathers over each eye. Their brown feathers were speckled with dots like snowflakes. The other owl, with the white face, was much larger. Her feathers were a lovely tawny color, but her eyes were as black as river stones. So black and so shiny that Tuki could see his own reflection. And his reflection made him sad. It made him miss his mama. The owls were nice. They were very soft. But when he saw his reflection and that of the female burrowing owl standing beside him, stroking his shoulders with her pretty wing, it reminded him of his mama's hands. He missed his mama's hands, which also stroked his shoulders and his cheeks and cupped his face in her palms and sang the good-night song. Nobody sang the good-night song here. They didn't sleep. They went flying about all night long, except whoever stayed behind to mind him. They did make a nice place for him to sleep. They plucked out the downiest fluff from the underside of their wings to make a bed for him. But it wasn't the same. It just wasn't the same.

"Do you smell it, Yazz? You have been with them more recently than I have," Hold On said. Yazz knew who "them" was. "Them" was the humans.

"I'm not sure," Yazz replied, twitching her long ears uneasily. "For a while I thought I did smell them, but then it faded."

"But now it's back. Isn't it?" Hold On could see a flicker of fear in the mule's large, dark eyes.

"Back but different? Don't you think?" Yazz asked.

The stallion paused. "Not so many perhaps, but one is enough."

"It's not just the number of them. Something else is different," Yazz replied.

It was the hottest part of the day. The herd was resting in the shade of what they had come to call lace trees, for the delicate leaves cast a shadow that reminded the two old mares of the lacy mantillas their mistresses wore. The air seemed thick and drowsy. The horses were almost asleep. The stallion and the mule moved off quietly.

Hold On picked up a perplexing sound, a sound he had to untangle from the gurgling of a brook. He could just make out the alternate whimpers and soft cries of a *baby*!

Hold On began to tremble. "There's a baby, a baby down by that creek." He took off at a trot, with Yazz close behind.

The baby was standing up in the shallow water, crying and shaking what appeared to be the rattles from a rattle-snake's tail. When the horse and the mule appeared, he opened his eyes wide with fear and screamed, "Mama!" Three owls were perched on a rock close by. The white-faced one stretched out her wing and began stroking the baby's head and making soft clucking sounds as if she were trying to soothe the child.

"This is unbelievable," Yazz said. "Can you see it at all, Hold On?"

"Yes, a little — but I can hear. A baby standing in a stream and an owl."

"Yes. What should we do? I know nothing about children."

"Get Tijo! Get him quickly." Hold On was panting as if he had been galloping hard. But he was standing still, quivering.

A few minutes later, Tijo arrived riding Estrella, with the rest of the herd trotting sleepily behind.

Toshi 'N Tuki looked up. These new animals were huge, like none he had ever seen before. He squatted down in the water, hiding beneath the *omo* owl's spread wings as he tried to make sense of these peculiar beasts, and then he spotted one that seemed to be a very odd assemblage of parts both animal and . . .

He gasped and threw his arms in the air.

"Tijo!" he cried.

Tijo leapt from Estrella's back and landed almost directly in the creek.

"Toshi 'N Tuki . . . Toshi 'N Tuki. What . . . what are you doing here?" He splashed toward the child and picked him up in his arms, hugging him tightly.

Quickly, Tijo mounted Estrella and tucked the child in front, holding him firmly. Toshi 'N Tuki clasped his arms around Tijo's waist and buried his head against his chest, weeping tears of joy and relief. He had been found.

Estrella slipped into a loping canter. Soon, Tuki's tears ceased, and lulled by gentle rhythms, he fell asleep. Soft snores issued from his tiny nose.

They brought Tuki back to their encampment. The horses were fascinated.

"Look at that little foal," Sky said.

"Just a tiny little colt," Verdad whinnied softly.

Then Angela stepped forward. "He's not a foal, and not a colt. He's a baby boy. Well, some might say a toddler. And the last time I saw a baby was at the baptism of the princess's son in the Old Land. Oh, he was dressed all in lace and had golden hair. But this one is just as lovely."

"But he's shivering!" Corazón said. "Get him a blanket."

The child was shivering from the cold water of the creek. Tijo wrapped him in a hide and fed him bits of the grouse jerky he had cured.

Speaking with Tuki was not so easy since Tijo had forgotten much of the Burnt River Clan tongue. And although Tuki was a very intelligent little boy, he did not have all the words needed to explain how the clan was moving north, or how he had become separated from them at a stream where his mother and the other women had gone to wash clothes.

Tijo finally turned to Hold On. "Can you find their scent?"

"I'll try." Although Hold On had spent most of his time in

the New World trying to avoid humans other than Tijo, he knew it was wrong to separate a young one from its dam.

So Hold On and Yazz went out that night. But Tuki would not let Tijo out of his sight. He curled up in Tijo's arms under the blanket. Tijo looked down at the child's lovely and perfectly round little face. He was at peace. The world that had been so scary and complicated for Tuki was once more safe and simple. Yet at the same time, it had become much more complicated for Tijo. He had to do what was right for the child. Return him to his people. But Tuki's people were no longer Tijo's people.

The horses heard Tijo humming the good-night song to the child, and the Boy Born with Luck on His Head felt safe and no longer thought the world had walked away from him. The vastness contracted. He felt the breath of Tijo as he sang and watched the stars appear, as if the night itself were listening to this lullaby.

Hold On and Yazz returned the next morning. Tijo was up as soon as he heard the sound of their hooves.

"Did you find them?"

"They are not that far." Yazz nodded. She had seen their sledges with the dogs in harnesses. It had unnerved her. These people did not know about horses yet or mules. Mules who could pull one hundred times the weight four dogs could pull. She would die before she was harnessed or yoked again.

"Did they see you?" Estrella asked.

"No," Yazz said.

"Are you sure?" Grullo asked.

"Yes, quite sure. They did not see us."

Then they all turned toward Tijo. He knew what they were thinking. Would he go back, back to the clan that had treated him so poorly? And he thought to himself, *They do not know the half of it*. They could not understand the cruelty of the healer.

"The *omo* owl!" Estrella said softly. Tijo tipped his head up and caught sight of her. He had told Estrella about the owl, but had she ever seen it?

And then as if she were reading his mind, she spoke. "I saw the owl. It was the owl who killed the coyote. And now here she is. You must go to the clan. You must take the child back to his people. To his mother."

Tijo knew she was right. There was no choice. He had to take the baby back. The *omo* owl at that moment felt once more a soft jolt in her gizzard. Her spirit lodger had returned for this journey. She spread her wings and lofted into the air from the stump where she perched, then settled on Tijo's shoulder. Tijo looked up into her black eyes. She blinked, and a light flashed deep within them, ancient and yet somehow familiar, as if from the farthest stars that burned in the night. It flashed again, and he recalled the first time he had seen the light. It was when she had picked him up from the side of the trail and cradled him in her arms.

"Haru?" he murmured. *Haru!*

CHAPTER 24

The Boy Older Than Time

The herd watched Tijo astride Estrella with Tuki and the *omo* owl flying above dissolve into the vapors of the early dawn. They knew this was the right thing to do. Every single one of them had suffered when they had been separated from their young or when the young like Sky and Verdad had been separated from their dams. Humans were different but in some ways perhaps not that different.

To the east a dust storm had swirled up, and its outrider whirlwinds danced across the horizon. As the sun rose higher, Tijo saw the shadow of the *omo* owl's wings printed against the hard-packed earth. Soon he recognized the tracks of the sledges of the clan. He caught the scent of their dogs. Footprints led into a gully where black sage grew, a plant favored for teas to treat stomach ailments. The signs of the people of the Burnt

River Clan were all around. There was nothing quiet about the way the clan traveled through the country. The terrain appeared hectic with their passage. And with each moment, he felt a deep, growing fear. The signs of their travel had a fretful clamor. He began to dread each step Estrella took. He clutched Tuki tighter.

Estrella was quiet as they rode and the baby, too, seemed very subdued and hardly shook the snake rattles that had quickly become a beloved toy. Every once in a while he would say a few words. "Mama . . . going to see Mama . . . Mama coming." And Tijo would reassure him. "Yes, I am taking you to your mama." The baby began asking, "How soon?" and Tijo would reply, "Soon, I think. Soon." For the tracks were becoming fresher.

And then ahead, Tijo saw the many-colored tablelands rising up in the distance. These sudden elevations of terrain with flat tops and steep cliffsides stippled the landscape. He had heard Haru speak of this place. Formerly, the Clan of the Red Corn had lived on these tablelands. A complicated labyrinth of canyons carved between these formations. Soon he glimpsed the winding ribbon of green, the river into which the creeks and streams of the canyons drained. The people of the Red Corn Clan had left. No one was sure why. Tijo approached, he could see that his clan, the Burnt River People, had already set up poles for their shelters.

The *omo* owl swooped down. But it was the voice of Haru

in his head. *This is the Place of Sliding Water, and they have begun already to build brush arbors.*

He signaled Estrella to slow down. A strange conversation began in his head. Sometimes the voices became tangled and he was unsure if it was himself speaking, questioning, or if it was Haru. And then sometimes it seemed as if there was the voice of Estrella.

What is my place? Is it clan or herd? These horses and the mule have treated me better than any human ever has except you, Haru.

You must decide. I cannot tell you.

But you always told me what to do.

You were a boy then.

I am still a boy.

You are not the same boy. You are a boy older than time.

Time weaver, is that what you are saying? But there was only silence now. Then more silence. He would try again.

Remember how they teased me? Remember the snare with the rattlesnakes, Hikyu's snare?

But look at Toshi 'N Tuki. He shakes the snake's rattles. They are his totem.

HIS TOTEM . . . HIS TOTEM . . . The words sang down Tijo's bones with an electrifying resonance.

The sky seemed to hang with dust and in the afterglow of the sunset the sandstone cliffs of the tablelands turned bloodred. Tiny dark figures melted out of the rock. They appeared like ants emerging from a sandhill at this distance. The totem, Tijo thought again, and reached behind Tuki for the bundle of coyote skin that he had rolled up. Estrella stopped so Tijo could slip it over his shoulders and set the coyote head atop his own. It covered his forehead down to his eyebrows. He touched the scar on his cheek, shaped by the wound he had stitched. He heard Tuki shake the rattles. *Two totems,* he thought.

They drew closer and closer. Nearly the entire clan was walking toward them, led by the healer, who wore a chieftain's headdress. It appeared to be identical to the one the last chieftain had worn. There were the antlers of a deer, from which hung the fangs of a mountain lion.

They were now within scant feet of one another. The people's eyes were wide with disbelief. The chieftain was holding his spear pointing down toward the ground, then suddenly he raised it. At the same moment, Toshi 'N Tuki peeked out from behind Tijo's back. A woman screamed and rushed forward. Estrella charged. The healer fell back, his spear clattering to the ground.

"Mama!" Tuki cried. Quickly, Tijo slid the child around so the mother could grab him. Then he signaled Estrella to walk up to the healer, who was still sprawled on the ground. Tijo looked down at him. The healer was clearly frightened.

Hikyu, his son, came forward and attempted to help his father get up, but the healer pushed his son's arm away. He staggered to his feet.

"Leave the spear!" Tijo said.

"Who are you?" the healer said. Clearly he did not recognize Tijo under the pelt and head of the coyote.

The *omo* owl hovered close and the people cowered. For it seemed that all things powerful, more powerful than the healer, were coming together. The ghostly owl, the pelt of the witch dog coyote, and the face marked by the claw of a bobcat.

"Who am I?" Tijo said. "I wear the pelt of the Trickster, but I am no trickster."

"Who are you?" the healer repeated. "And what is this creature you ride on?"

Tijo flipped back his head so that the coyote head fell away, revealing his face.

"*Look!*" Hikyu shouted out. "It's Lame Boy, that's all."

The *omo* owl swooped down from the sky and knocked Hikyu to the ground. In the same instant, Estrella reared up, pawing the air. Tijo lifted his arms to the sky. "I am Horse Boy. That is my name. Call me Horse Boy."

There was a mighty thud as Estrella's hooves struck the ground. Then she spun around, breaking into a gallop that left the people dazzled by her beauty and speed. They watched in silence as Horse Boy became no more than a shadow on the horizon, then faded completely.

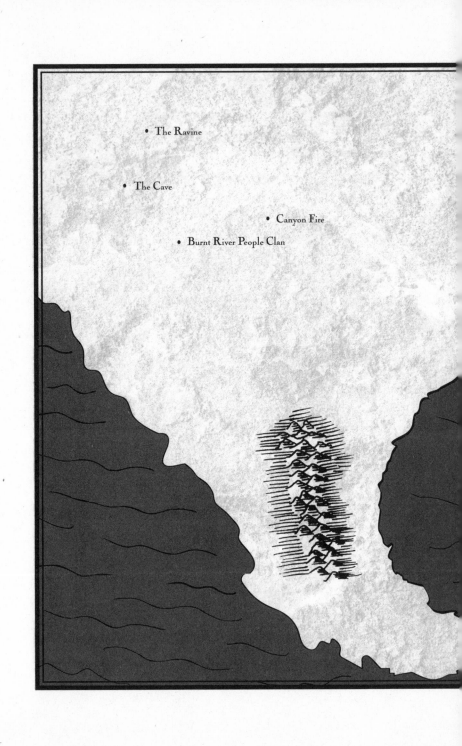

About the Author

Kathryn Lasky is the author of the bestselling Guardians of Ga'Hoole series, which has more than seven and a half million copies in print, as well as the Wolves of the Beyond series. Her books have received a Newbery Honor, a Boston Globe–Horn Book Award, and a Washington Post–Children's Book Guild Award. She lives with her husband in Cambridge, Massachusetts.